success

Steve Backley OBE

The Champion in All of Us
12 rules for success

Steve Backley OBE
The only British track & field athlete to win medals at three different Olympic Games.

First edition
Published in Great Britain
By Mirage Publishing 2012

Text Copyright © Steve Backley 2012

First published in paperback 2012

A CIP catalogue record for this book
Is available from the British Library.

ISBN: 978-1-90257-8781

Mirage Publishing
PO Box 161
Gateshead
NE8 4WW
Great Britain

Printed and bound in Great Britain by

Book Printing UK

For every coach, physio, doctor, therapist, scientist, teacher, training partner and all the support staff around them. The continual support and assistance from experts who never gain the credit they deserve made it possible for me to pursue my dreams and I am eternally grateful. They are all champions and worthy of the highest place on any rostrum.

There is, however, one coach who taught me more deeply than I can ever express. He had an impact on my development before and then throughout my career and continues to offer great support, and that is my father, John Backley.

Contents

Disclaimer

This is a work of fiction. Any similarity between characters within and persons living or dead is entirely coincidental. Representation of real names, places, occurrences, or persons, living or dead, is not intended and should not be inferred. Characters, names, locals, and events depicted are either the artistic creation of the author or are used fictitiously.

The publisher, the author, the distributors and bookstores present this information for entertainment purposes only. Any exercises presented herein, either physical or mental, are to be followed with caution.

You and only you are responsible if you choose to do anything based on what you read.

Preface

If your focus is performance — either for yourself, your team or that of your organisation — then this tale of four athletes seeking success and chasing their dreams, can assist you and your team to reach your full potential.

The journey of four athletes and their passion to succeed are used to symbolise deeper meaning through the practical philosophy of twelve rules for achieving greater performance.

This is about much more than the power of positive thinking; look out for the correlation in your life, because it will challenge you to look deeply into your own performance and to contemplate the impact you may have on that of others. This book, whatever your walk of life — whether in sport, business or in everyday life — is a maze of ideas aimed at anyone who has a dream and a passion to succeed.

For those to whom success comes from inspiring and assisting in the improved performance of others, the irresistible and memorable teachings in this book will make a great deal of sense.

This is a journey into the most important challenges facing us all. It is a cohesion of ideas that puts forward an inspirational framework which can promote self-confidence, inspire change and develop a passion to commit to your dreams.

The Characters

The four athletes

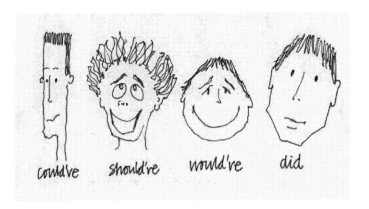

could've should're would've did.

It was the end of the closing ceremony of the Olympic Games. As the dust settled, all the athletes returned to the Olympic village, where statements reverberated regarding their performances ....

Some had delivered exceptionally – done themselves justice and others were left to contemplate what had happened and what they might have done differently.

"I could have done better ...."

"I should have done more ...."

"I would have medalled, but ...." and

"I did try my hardest ...."

Elsewhere, at this very moment, watching on, four new, young athletes were born – *Could've, Should've Would've and Did.*

Years later....

The four grew up and became dedicated athletes — sprinters. Whilst they came from the four corners of the country, all had been born with a level of talent and a common goal. They had all grown up winning their local sprinting events and had gone through the ranks like many had, from school to club, to regional, to country wide success. This was just the beginning.

Each athlete had made a commitment to pursue their dreams; they had all seen the Olympics on TV as kids and marvelled at the intensity and passion from the athletes they watched competing as though their lives depended on it.

They have come together to train both as individuals and to be part of a group; all four have the same dream: not only of being a great sprinter, but of, maybe, one day being the fastest man on earth. Each of them has unique characteristics but they are all very different.

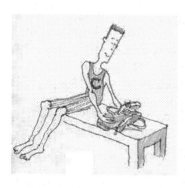

Could've – a tall, lean, smart and strong athlete is the type of person who understands and likes other people, but who challenges them. Compared to the other three athletes, he came to the sport late in life, which has created self-limiting beliefs in his mind as to whether he can catch up.

Rather than seeing how much potential he has, he always stops short of creating and maintaining a great performance due to his limiting beliefs, self-doubt and a general lack of trust in himself.

The Champion in all of Us

Could've doesn't know it yet, but it is his inherent lack of self-belief that is his major weakness.

Did – tried many sports as a child growing up, but he wasn't a great athlete through his early years and hadn't been very successful; his failures far outweighing his triumphs.

Did has to work harder than the others, but knows that he can fight when needed. To *Did*, the others seem confident and, in many ways, more talented than him.

Did knows that he will really need to listen to his coach to get the best out of himself. He feels fortunate to be in such a positive environment and is prepared to do whatever it takes. He chooses to be proactive, focused and disciplined.
He is committed to exploring his potential; in some ways,

Did's drive and determination stem from his lack of inherent ability. In his case, not being very physically talented would have an upside.

While there are a number of barriers for Did to overcome in order to realise his full potential, he will come to understand that his success will come from mirroring the behaviour and methods of others.

Should've – was a child superstar, always excelling as a youngster, breaking records and, in some ways, he had it easy.

He knows what makes him great and is happy with those ways and methods that he believes are tried and tested.

Should've is of the opinion that he really doesn't need to explore new ways but has now, reluctantly, joined the group after his previous trainer moved on.

With his overly developed sense of optimism, *Should've* knows that he may even teach any *Coach* a thing or two.

Should've is unaware, at this stage of his development, that it is his inability to seek and initiate change that will ultimately hold him back.

Would've – a great all rounder who probably 'would have' made it in any sport. During a recent competition he enjoyed the company of *Should've* and *Could've* so much that he came to join the group more out of curiosity than anything else.

His biggest challenge is his lack of passion and motivation for the sport. *Would've*, to the casual observer, seems to work hard but is actually often criticised for just going through the motions.

Through self-indulgence and self–centredness he lacks passion, which doesn't instil a desire to grow. In essence, he lacks the mindset, self–awareness and discipline to achieve full momentum – but he has the potential for incredible transformation.

Would've simply lacks the desire, the enthusiasm and the will to commit with all his heart.

Clearly, they were all talented in their own ways and had come from different backgrounds in order to seek the advice of the man who was going to help them reach their dreams. His name was *Coach*.

The Facilitator of the Twelve Rules

Coach – is wise and always knows what to do; he plans well and is able to deal with problems with a calm and comprehending nature. More significantly, he is inspirational to be around because he shares his philosophies, he listens and he leads by example; most importantly, he is determined to get the best out of the four athletes he is about to take under his wing.

Coach is no ordinary teacher of sport; he is a man of significant pedigree and commands great respect from both athletes and other coaches alike. This respect comes not only from the success he has delivered as a coach, but from his deeper understanding of performance. He has studied the concept of winning and sees this as a science. He spends many hours poring over literature on the subject and meeting with champions, past and present, to look for insights and commonalities in them.

Coach has lived all over the world spending his apprentice years interpreting for the best coaches in Russia, then Eastern Europe and the States. Honing his own methods, he amassed knowledge as he went. This has given him a great depth of understanding into various aspects of development around not only the skills and the techniques required to be a champion but, more importantly, an understanding of how to develop others' performance through teaching them how to apply themselves effectively. This is the secret of *Coach*'s success – his ability to optimise a person's potential.

His ethos, inspired by a compilation of everything he has learned, is not to create change, but to create *lasting change.*

Coach also knows that the faults you see in others are often the reflection of faults within yourself, and that conversely, it is equally true that the strengths you see in others are the untapped abilities you possess within, and this is how he will work with the team.

He has always had the ability to tap into, exploit and develop what is possible for every athlete he works with, and has a framework that would allow others to do the same through the various performance–rules he has developed in twelve individual, simple lessons which form *Coach*'s rules for success. His challenge, as a coach, was to be able to instil these to become part of the DNA of each of his athletes' behavioural make–up.

Coach will use his wisdom and his performance model to steer his charges towards taking chances and getting uncomfortable; in doing so he will reveal to each of them their full potential.

The first step is to help the group appreciate who they are, open their minds up to new possibilities, take them on a journey of personal development and maybe, just maybe, reach their dreams.

The Olympics

The Games – less than two years away, and *Coach* knows the importance of getting to work quickly.

All four of the athletes had demonstrated their talent by making the finals of the National Championship in the previous year and were likely to be selected for international competitions this coming year. The final hurdle for them all, to ultimately make it on the big stage – the Olympic stage – was to step up: to go from being an ordinary athlete, to a contender, to becoming a champion. This, a word that *Coach* did not use lightly, refers to the behaviour of an individual as opposed to the outcome. *Coach* had met many champions, all with winning mindsets, and he enjoyed learning about and understanding their behaviour; some had won too.

Interestingly, he also views this same mindset in champions outside of sport, people who lead in their field and are considered the most effective at achieving their goals. To *Coach,* it was clear that these well–formed and effective behaviour traits were apparent from sprinting to business management, from a gymnast to an entrepreneur, or a golfer to a banker.

The Secret Coach

The start of the dream

It was a typical Tuesday evening at the athletics training track. There were high–jumpers at one end of the track and hammer throwers at the other, taking it in turns to release the hammer out into the centre of the grass area on the infield.

There was a range of talent on display, runners, jumpers and throwers. In particular, however, were four athletes who were different; the four didn't understand it yet but they were all going to be presented with an opportunity to develop themselves in a perfect training environment and maybe reach their dreams of going to – and succeeding at – the Olympic Games.

On this early autumn evening, the four were going about some typical pre–winter basic training, the sort of work that all athletes do to improve their basic fitness and athleticism. Long slow repetitions on the track, circuits and other low–impact repetitious work off it. This grounding would prepare them for the more intense, specific work, later in the training cycle in the months to come.

The summer seemed a distant memory and the team were aware of the impending work that they'd all need to do as winter drew closer. The leaves on the track seemed to remind them of this, and their warmer tracksuits were out in preparation for it, the first and most gritty part of their yearly cycle.

Observing the athletes from the otherwise empty stand was a nondescript man who, on first sight, looked to be in his sixties. This visit was *Coach*'s first close–up encounter with his prodigies: *Could've, Should've, Would've* and *Did*.

The athletes went about their day's training and it was clear to all that there was a similar level of ability in the group, which would make things interesting for whoever was ready to take the reins and help them to explore their capabilities. As he looked on, they all seemed to be very quick and had the raw talent that would be a prerequisite, given their chosen path.

Throughout his long career, *Coach* had plenty of hands–on coaching experience. Many years prior he had himself been an athlete, but had never really made it to the top flight of sport. He had shown some promise in his early twenties, when he made international level, but his career was cut short due to a car accident which resulted in serious back problems; this had left *Coach* with a real passion to help others. One of the reasons *Coach* could offer the group so much was that he knew the hurt of not being able to reach what his own potential really was.

Coach referred to a small set of notes he had received from each of the athletes' previous coaches; this together with his ever watchful and experienced eyes, even from a distance that evening, began to decipher their skills, and their capabilities.

As the group stretched off after the session, *Coach* approached them and introduced himself. They all shook hands and greeted each other with a warm smile. Little was said, but there was a powerful atmosphere of positive uncertainty and anticipation.

Even through these first few minutes of superficial chat, *Coach* quickly reinforced what he had learned from their previous coaches' notes and had begun to assess further as he had sat and watched.

Could've

The most evident was *Could've*'s lack of self-belief. His previous coach had written "*... in order to maximise his potential, Could've needs to learn to trust and believe in himself.*"

Coach had met athletes like this before and knew exactly what to do. He was confident that he could assist *Could've* in this progression. The only question was whether *Could've* would buy in to *Coach*'s mantra that 'if you don't believe you can do something, you never will succeed'. *Coach* ran the words through his head, "If you don't believe in yourself, why should anybody else believe in you?"

He knew from past experience that you cannot allow yourself any limiting or negative thoughts and beliefs that will prevent you from accomplishing your goals.

Coach was able to see and feel what this would look like and how he could improve this in *Could've* and smiled at the clarity this gave him – a vision and the beginnings of a plan.

Should've

Coach learned from the notes provided by his previous coach that *Should've* was reluctant to explore new options. He wore the same style of clothes, day in and day out, and took the exact same journey to the track where he trained every day.

He would turn up at exactly the same time, and went through the very same routine each day. He would go to the same spot at the low fence around the track, do the same stretches in the same order and have the same conversations.

Coach made a mental note that outlined how he would steer *Should've* towards creating the changes in his life that would help him become a champion.

Coach liked routine but knew that, done to this degree, it could be limiting to an athlete like *Should've*. He also knew that to aspire to be the greatest, *Should've* would need to accept change and take on what he might perceive to be risk.

Coach realised that, in order to be a champion, *Should've* needed to undergo a series of new experiences to alter how he perceived change. And how, if he chose to, he could take control of his future by initiating these changes as he developed.

He understood the consequences of being 'change-phobic'. It would take either a huge gain or huge pain to get *Should've* out of this destructive mindset. He had an idea ... and, ultimately, it would change *Should've*'s life.

Would've

 *Coach* had learned from the notes that *Would've* lacked passion; he was happy where he was – and *Coach* could see there was no hunger in his eyes. *Would've* already had his 'ticket to the party' and was too busy enjoying himself to worry about being a champion, mainly because he already felt that he was one. *Coach* understood this and knew that he needed to help *Would've* find his passion to enable him to fully realise his talent.

Coach knew that to get to the bottom of *Would've*'s problems, he would need to understand him on a much deeper level than he had in just a brief chat. *Coach* set out to do just this, but he knew that it would take time; fortunately, he was a patient and passionate man himself.

Did

Coach learned that his previous coach "… saw greatness, but also a single-mindedness that, while effective for his own performance, could prove destructive to the team."

Coach knew the power of the 'team'. He wanted *Did* to learn about the power of wider responsibility and committing to the group. This was going to be *Coach*'s biggest challenge: to help *Did* move from independence to interdependence.

Coach liked the fact that *Did* wanted to take responsibility for himself, but wanted him to get to the very top and knew that he would need help from others in order to make it. To get *Did* to appreciate, learn and take ownership of this important shift was *Coach*'s goal.

Coach was ready to begin his work, to introduce, in sequence, his twelve rules for success and to take his four athletes on an amazing journey of development.

Rule 1

Champions Decide to Work Hard

New mountains to climb

After the evening's training was over, *Coach* joined the four athletes at a meeting in the clubhouse to introduce his intentions more formally.

"It gives me great pleasure to act as your new coach. Until the Games I will be your advisor, your confidant, your trusted servant and probably the most challenging person you will have ever met. I will develop a master plan and this will gradually unfold over the coming two years. You will also have your own personal development plan which will run alongside the general work that you will do together as a group. While there is this plan, you will inevitably need to adapt to circumstances that will inevitably arise along the way."

Coach wanted to ease the athletes into his mindset, so he explained, "While it is always important to plan, it is equally important to be flexible. You don't just have to think outside of the box, you sometimes have to get out of the box."

Should've became anxious that his routines would be messed around, and didn't like this; he said, "Can I have a set plan, one I can stick to?" To his mind, it would be safer.

In his head, *Coach* asked, "What are you afraid of, *Should've*?"

Outwardly, *Coach* explained, "Although I understand that you'd like a set routine, it is important to remain open to adaptations that might improve the plan along the way.

Assess, Adapt and Evolve, is a phrase I will use often. If you constantly *assess* effectively and then *evolve* by *adapting* appropriately, you will continue to improve. This will throw up the need for some flexibility from you."

Since *Should've* had openly voiced his concerns, the eyes of the three other athletes were firmly fixed on *Coach*; they had already picked up on his reaction in explaining that a rigid routine is not always practical.

Coach sensed that if he faltered now, then that is how he would be forever remembered by the athletes, so he needed to make his mark in a powerful yet empowering way. His authority had to be respected otherwise he would have difficulty in securing success for the group as they would lose their sense of cohesion.

Coach knew that most people don't like it when others try to boss them about and that it is far easier to energise people and get them to see a common vision through empowerment, as opposed to ordering them around, and he knew that empowerment would get the best response from these athletes.

Coach had that 'deep in thought' look as he shifted his gaze from the floor, surveying and weighing up each one of the group in turn. He paused for a few seconds, knowing he would need something big to get their attention, and started, "Have you ever wondered why some people are so lucky? The kind of person that has everything going for them, for whom things work out just fine, no matter what they do? They have a first-class relationship, a top job in their chosen profession: things just seem to go their way. It's as though luck is always on their side.

"Now let me explain the secret as to why they are so lucky and, in so doing, I'll show you how you can create the same kind of good luck out of thin air."

This was a big claim from *Coach* who had set out to get

their attention, and he had certainly fired their interest.

Coach went on, "What if I were to tell you hundreds of people were studied over a decade to see if good luck played a part in their lives? What this study revealed was the answer to the riddle of how you think and how you see things, both of which are responsible for good things happening to you.

"Simply altering the way you think can set your own good luck and good fortune in motion. I want you to get curious as to what you could be."

Momentarily holding *Should've*'s eyes with a fixed but friendly gaze, *Coach* continued, "People are lucky because they take hold of a chance; they construct positive, self–fulfilling prophecies and have a positive attitude that allows them to turn bad luck into good luck by focusing on what they want, right?"

Should've started nodding his head, as did each other member of the group in agreement.

Coach went on, "Instead of complaining, they're thankful for whatever happened and look to take the positive out of any negative.

"Just like those 'lucky' people, you too can begin to change your fortune and create your own good luck, not just by training your body, but also by training your mind to be more positive, more optimistic, more aware of opportunities, and as a consequence you can achieve self–created good fortune.

"Over the coming months, I'm going to introduce you to some ideas that will help you to become more positive.

"If you want to create your own good luck then you have to hold an open mind; this means that you take a closer look at the opportunities available to you.

"If you want to become a stronger athlete and someone who commands respect, this requires a worthwhile investment of your time. Explore it. Unlucky people are simply unlucky because they miss opportunities; they're not open to new possibilities and feel they have to do things a certain way.

"Lucky people will focus on what's in front of them rather than scrabbling about for what they're searching for."

Then, briefly looking at each of the group in turn, *Coach* raised his voice slightly and announced, "*Could've*, you need to believe in your gifts. *Should've*, you need to be open to all possibilities. *Would've*, you need to start living up to your expectations. And finally, *Did*, you need to draw strength from the others.

"Oh, and as for me, I need to work my socks off helping you to reach your potential as winners!"

The athletes were really engaged through *Coach*'s insightful knowledge, but he wasn't finished yet. "Try a change of approach when you can. Do things a little differently. When you do this frequently you get both your conscious and subconscious mind to focus on discovering new ways to do things.

"That's when luck starts to come your way. It's all because your subconscious mind begins to generate the circumstances for you to succeed. But this will only come about when you believe you can have good luck and when you believe that you can succeed.

"You can start to change your luck today. Begin believing that you can have what you desire and superior things will arrive."

Directing his gaze back to *Should've*, *Coach* said in a rich and friendly voice, "Oh, and just in case you're wondering how most of those in the self-limiting study group started to experience an improved success rate ... well, it came about for them when they became more open-minded, more positive and started doing things differently."

Everyone was now showing an intense interest. *Coach*

focused his attention on the whole group and continued, "A few simple changes led to a better life and created good luck while doing away with the perceived bad luck. It sounds so simple, and it is. For some people, however, changing the way they do things, seeing possibilities and being more open-minded when they're not used to being that way, focusing on good fortune instead of bad luck, changing their routines and trying a different approach is so different from what they're used to doing that they simply can't change. Why? Because they slip into unwanted habits due to familiarity.

"Typically, habits dominate people and then they feel unable to change – why? Well it's simply because they choose to allow this to happen. So, what should you do? Start changing and breaking the unwanted habits, and in so doing create new habits that work for you and allow you to create the kind of luck that you want."

Coach searched for the vibe of the group so he could tap into their thoughts; this would help him understand the prevailing views.

All felt they wanted more but it was *Did* who spoke up, "How do we start this?"

Coach went on, "Explore. Train your conscious mind and your subconscious mind to start working for you by getting those great powers to move in a new direction. Start creating your own good luck today.

"Remember, if you don't do anything – if you don't change the way your mind works and direct your subconscious mind to create the life you want – then everything stays the same, nothing changes. This is *your* life: make the most of it."

When *Coach* had finished his talk, all four athletes were silent, reflecting on their own behaviour. *Coach* clapped his hands lightly together to clear the air, stepped back and said,

"Right, they don't give Olympic medals out for talking a good game!"

With the tension of the first official meeting gone, *Coach* felt good as he had made an impact on the group. As they were saying their goodbyes and heading off, though, he added: "Oh, just a few words before you all go. From what I could see from the spectator stand, it was a great session today. I get the feeling that the dynamic of this group is going to take you all a long way. You all have an incredible potential." *Coach* then paused slightly longer than was comfortable ...

Going by how *Coach* had spoken to them in the short time they had spent so far and now the subtle shift in his body language, the four athletes knew something significant was about to be said.

Coach pulled himself up to his full height: he wasn't overly tall, but it gave him an assertive stance that enhanced his physical presence. This was his characteristic posture whenever he was about to say something of great importance. His demeanour became one of substance. Now the athletes could see that he had the presence of someone who meant business – the mood in the group changed

"Over the next couple of years, I will have lots of important messages for you, but that what I am about to say now is probably the most important lesson I can ever offer; it is critical to your success."

Coach drew a breath and said with calmness, "I want to share with you the first of many rules. It is the most simple and straightforward rule, probably something that you already know, but in its simplicity comes wonderful clarity. I must know that you understand this, the basic, non-negotiable rule which is a pre-requisite for any success."

Coach then shared his first rule ....

RULE 1
Champions Decide to Work Hard

"Successful academics study hard, and businessmen who make it to the very top also work hard. If you want to be a champion you'll naturally want to get up for the early training sessions and get going, without thinking twice about it; you'll never see working hard as a chore.

"To deliver your own personal maximum, you'll realise there are no shortcuts; if you want to be a champion it is all about rolling your sleeves up and getting stuck in. In simple terms, champions decide to work hard! You'll also need to expect a high level of performance from your colleagues, and encourage them to keep up with you."

Coach took a long pause ... before continuing.

To enhance his message, he was about to test them in an environment which was out of their normal routine.

"Tomorrow, I would like to do something a little different from what you have been doing recently. I'd like you all to join me for a great day out: walking, in one of my favourite places ... the mountains."

There was a mountain range a short drive from the training track, and it had a number of rugged, winding and testing paths by way of which you could reach the peaks. Some of the paths were very challenging and would require the agility of a mountain goat and great strength to climb them; a place where high winds and rain increased the peril of the rocky ascent.

This would be the perfect environment for their first – and possibly most important – test, for he knew they would struggle. But *Coach* was only interested in one thing: *how they would cope with struggling.*

*****

Coach loved to do these testing walks in his free time and, as a result, was fit enough to tackle it. The group however, as power athletes, were not, and *Coach* knew this. He knew that that their fast-contracting, fast–fatiguing muscles were not designed for long walks. Early in the training cycle, *Coach* saw this varied approach, to build a good foundation of basic conditioning, whilst testing their ability to cope with pain, sustaining effort and overcoming adverse conditions, as ideal.

"I'd like you all to meet me here at 5am with walking footwear and a backpack. Bring enough water to last the day, I suggest four litres or so, and I'll bring food." Then he paused, looked into their eyes and asked, "Are you all in then?"

Should've hated change, he had never done anything like this before that would take him away from his trusted training schedule – so he wanted to decline.

However, like most of the rest of the group, he didn't speak up, for the way *Coach* had presented the request made each of them feel obliged to go along with it. They felt that they could not decline: this would be disrespectful to *Coach* as he, for some reason, saw this as an important outing.

Would've welcomed the idea. He saw this as a chance to break the monotony of the track-work they had been doing. "Brilliant. How far are we going?"

"Just be ready for a long, hard day and you'll be fine," *Coach* replied without letting too much out of the bag.

Could've through his lack of self–belief struggled to see the relevance. "Is it not a bit unsafe to climb those mountains? I have always been told not to go there," he said, shakily.

Coach confidently replied, "You'll be fine with me," adding, with emphasis, "Sometimes we have to take calculated risks and explore new ideas. And anyway, it will be a lot of fun."

"Fun," groaned *Could've*. "I feel sick at the thought."

Deep down, *Should've* did trust *Coach* but found himself confused as to how to react because he'd slipped back into his habits. You see, he always woke at 7.30am, had a shower at the same time, always had the same breakfast and always followed this same routine each day.

He wasn't sure how this day would work and asked, "Why so early?"

"Why not?" *Coach* replied.

Coach knew that *Should've* would question things due to his reluctance to accept new ways. He had expected him to be resistant to this change.

"It is the most beautiful part of the day and, more importantly, the part of the day that you will need to be at your level best to cope with the bigger competitions. Do you want to explore if you can be at your best at this time of the day?" *Coach* challenged.

"Well, yeah, but, you can't, can you?" replied *Should've*, before continuing, "Isn't there lots of evidence to prove that this is not possible?"

"Evidence!" chortled *Coach*, "Now, there's an interesting word."

This was the concept that *Coach* knew was pivotal to the group's development, for 'evidence' was the one thing that controlled each of the athletes' belief systems.

Also, 'explore' wasn't in *Should've*'s vocabulary either. He couldn't see the point … yet.

Coach continued, "I like the fact that you search for 'evidence'. So, with this in mind, what is the right question?" This baffled the group.

Could've walked away and inside he doubted *Coach*. He waited for the others to disperse and then as *Should've* approached he said, "So that's it, I travel across the country for cutting edge training and I have to get up at 5.00am and go on a walk. What's all that about?"

"See you all in the morning," *Coach* called out, as the group was now making a hasty retreat in case he had anything else up his sleeve.

Could've   Should've   Would've   Did

The group sloped further away. *Could've* felt anxious at the perceived danger. *Should've* felt awkward with the need to change his routine. *Would've* felt a little aggrieved at having to get up early, but looked forward to something different as he always got bored easily. *Did* left buzzing with excitement and wanted to know more.

The following morning, *Could've* was the first to arrive at the clubhouse.

"Morning, *Could've*," said a cheerful, wide-awake *Coach*.

Could've said nothing.

Coach knew that he was struggling with the idea of doing something so spontaneous. He knew that there was doubt in *Could've*'s mind as to the relevance of the exercise, and he understood that *Could've* needed reference — a set of values in order to be able to regulate his behaviour and to be able to really believe and commit to anything. This was exactly why they were there, away from their familiar surroundings.

With a reassuring smile, *Coach* asked, "I wonder, could you be interested in letting go of the things that hold you back and slow you down, as maybe now is the perfect time? Some of those negative experiences you're holding on to can be released, discarded and dumped into the trash along with yesterday's newspaper.

"I know from experience that just thinking about those negative events really slows you down. It destroys any chance of success and happiness; so really, there's no need to hang on to them.

"Being consumed by those feelings will destroy any chance of success because you're living in the past. I know moving forward is easier said than done, but today you will learn something really special."

Coach knew that what lay ahead was something that would work towards developing *Could've*'s ability to let go of unwanted events, emotions and situations – past or present – that were holding him back ... and then he could begin moving forward.

While they were waiting for the others to turn up, *Coach* looked around the car park and as he zoomed in on the rather large decorative stones meant to keep cars off the grass verge he said to *Could've*, "See that big stone over there," pointing to one of them, "will you bring it over here?"

Could've groaned. "Why?"

"Just humour me."

Could've had a feeling he was being made to feel small, and that this was just some ploy to keep him in his place, but he grudgingly obliged and soon the stone – which weighed about a quarter of his own body weight – was at *Coach*'s feet.

"Now," *Coach* instructed, pointing to another stone, "bring that one over here too."

Could've was gasping as he brought the second, even heavier stone to *Coach* and dropped it by his side, reproaching himself for expending so much energy so early on in the day.

Coach then said, "Walk to where you brought the last stone from and just walk back here again, but without gathering any stones this time."

Could've humoured *Coach* and obliged. When he had finished the task *Coach* said to him, "Did you find it easier walking without the dead weight draining you?" and, without waiting for an answer, continued, "Chances are you're like most people and you have a number of unpleasant experiences that you're holding on to. Just like when you were carrying those heavy stones, these experiences drain you of your energy and slow you down. All that weight on your mind is ten times heavier than those rocks, believe me.

"The more weight you carry, the worse life gets. It's that simple. You're carrying useless baggage which slows you down and burns away your valuable energy, so when you want to dig deep, there's nothing there.

"Along the road of life, *Could've*, you keep picking up heavy objects, things that really don't serve you, but, nevertheless, you want to hang on to them. After a while these objects begin to weigh down on you, and unless you get rid of them you'll never get to where you want to go.

"You can begin to let go by simply allowing your mind to focus on something different, just like when you walked back from where you got the last stone from. You forgot about your pain because you wondered what this was all about. You were distracted.

"Think of positive events. Think of positive experiences. Think about how you want to improve your life and start taking steps to make the changes.

"Doing this pushes your mind in a new direction and gives your subconscious mind a new set of instructions.

"Today you can start letting go, just like you let go of that last heavy stone. That will help, but if you really want to start moving on then you have to get your mind to focus on new things and, in the process, you automatically let go of the negative events and situations that have been slowing you down."

"How do I do that then?" *Could've* muttered.

"You have to ask yourself, 'Where do I want to go now? How do I plan to get there?' You may not have the answers to these questions, but merely thinking about your options and your future, without carrying the heavy stones of the past, empowers your mind to get creative and go in new directions. When you do this you automatically let go of unwanted feelings and emotions."

Coach condensed all that he had said to *Could've*, "Start focusing on what you want to happen. Let go of the past and of negative situations by focusing your mind on new, different things. Direct your subconscious mind to help you let go by giving it new instructions.

"Remember – you only get one life, but hundreds, even thousands, of chances and it is up to you how you convert these chances. Do you understand?" he said to *Could've*.

Could've nodded in an understanding way.

Coach continued, "Even though you can't go back and change the past, you can influence the future. Make the most of it. Stop defeating yourself, stop limiting yourself. Create the success you want and deserve in life. And you know the best bit – you can start today!"

Just as *Coach* finished speaking, *Would've* and *Did* arrived. Because *Should've* was not an *early* person, it came as no surprise that he was the last to arrive.

Just before *Coach* ushered the group into the car he said to *Could've*, "Oh, would you mind replacing those rocks back where you got them from."

Could've felt self–conscious of doing this in front of the rest of the group, but *Coach* wanted to see how he reacted.

After *Could've* made a drama out of this task, he noticed *Should've* was carrying a rather large bottle of water in his hands and nothing else.

"Where's your backpack?" *Coach* asked *Should've*.

Should've shrugged. *Coach* opened the boot of his car and handed him a spare he'd brought along, as he had a feeling one or two of them would forget. As they set off for the foot of the mountain region, there was an ominous silence in the car.

Could've felt uneasy, and a little nervous – this came from his low self–belief. *Should've* felt decidedly uncomfortable with this unexpected set of events, as it was different, and *Would've* simply fell asleep as he was very tired: he had stayed up late, watching sport on TV. *Did* was intrigued; he wanted to ask *Coach* some questions but felt that the silence was appropriate ahead of what seemed like it might be a long and interesting day.

As soon as they arrived *Coach* asked each athlete to open their backpacks and placed in a weighty, bubble-wrapped package, saying, "These are little extras for you. I want you to consider them to be your friends. Now, put your 'friend' safely in your backpack.

"What I have given you may seem like an extra weight ...."

Could've, feeling hard done–by due to lifting the stones earlier on, began grumbling about this extra weight he would be carrying.

Coach interrupted him: "Thank you for questioning this, *Could've*. This friend will make you mountain fit. It will take you each to a place that I hope is beyond your comfort zone. Now that you know this, it will become apparent at a later date why I asked you to carry this extra weight."

Coach knew that, right at this moment, his reasoning would likely to be lost on the four, but later it would become clear that this zone of discomfort would be stored in each athlete's emotional memory, which would serve them well when they needed to draw on past experiences to help them through a tough spot.

Along with the rock, *Coach* had also placed a notepad and pen in each of their backpacks — another cunning plan.

"Let's go!" *Coach* called out, trying to hide his grin.

He set out up the first hill at a very quick, blistering pace, ahead of the four athletes. They tucked in behind him, still uncertain exactly what they could expect.

Coach knew they would struggle with this task, for it was not in their comfort zone. He purely wanted to see how each of the four would react to a difficult situation, and who was not willing to get uncomfortable when it came to working hard. *Coach* knew that this cautiousness is often what stops us from exploring, developing and maximising our potential.

Did kept pace with *Coach* and quizzed him about his previous athletes and how they had responded to his ways, "Have you always been able to get the best out of your athletes?

Coach told him, "There was once an athlete in my group who was maybe one of the most talented I have ever seen. However, he had one crucial part of the basics missing; he was lazy."

Coach slowed down so that the whole group were within earshot. He then repeated this line to make sure they all heard it. "He could have been a champion, but he had one crucial factor missing ... he was lazy.

"When the going got tough, he simply did not like it. You see, the cumulative effect of this over time is such that the lack of intent multiplies against you. Working hard every day is essential at this level – unproductive laziness results in failure.

"There was another athlete in one of my groups who was a real grinder. And there is a real, positive benefit to this type of productive behaviour over time.

"You see, the snowball effect of working hard every day builds momentum – a continuum. This is a gradual transition from one condition to a different condition, without any abrupt changes.

"When you near your maximum, you are asking your body to respond, to adapt. To improve, the training that is most effective is when it is difficult. I'd like you to explore this point, this point when you are close to failing through fatigue or being overloaded. In training terms, it is called 'reaching' or 'stretching'. It is essential that you befriend this zone of effort. I refer to this as the 'adaptation zone'; the phase of effort where you are accessing your potential. You will be spending much time in this space over the coming months. I'd like you to understand what it feels like, how you respond to it and how you can eventually take control of it.

"I want to be clear on this, the rest of the training leading up to this zone is essential in getting you there, it's once things get tough that it gets interesting. The adaptation zone is the place where champions are built. This applies to all aspects of personal development."

With this said, *Coach* let *Did* take the lead and followed behind him. Because what *Coach* had said made so much sense to *Did*, he was filled with enthusiasm. He wanted to get going and, as a result, quickened the pace slightly.

The group were thoughtful in their silence. *Should've* frowned at the change of pace as he had only just found his rhythm. *Could've* questioned in his mind whether this 'adaptation zone' theory might be a load of old rubbish. *Would've* went along with it all as he was kind of enjoying his day out, but he wondered if he'd be back in time for the football.

Fifteen minutes into the walk.... *Coach* stopped abruptly. "Oh no! I've left the map in the car. Would one of you run back and get it?" he asked.

"Ha, it was really tough getting this far. Run back! Do we need it?" *Could've* said in a tone of defiance.

Would've slid out of the way and pretended to enjoy the views while this got sorted out.

"I'll go," said a cheerful *Did*.

"Okay, thanks," *Coach* replied.

He had wanted the group to see that *Did* would react positively, just as *Coach* knew he would.

"Ask the others who'd like to come with you," *Coach* whispered in *Did*'s ear as he gave him the keys to his car.

"Who's coming with me?" *Did* asked eagerly.

"I need to rest," pleaded *Should've*.

"We'll time you," said *Would've*.

"I'll come," said *Could've*, who was disappointed in himself for not replying first, just as *Did* had.

Could've and *Did* left and *Coach* sat with the others and told them more about the two athletes in his previous group, the one who was lazy and the other who worked hard, and how the athlete who, on the face of it, was less talented but chose to work hard became the more successful.

Before long *Could've* and *Did* were back with the map and rejoined the group.

They set off on their ascent again, and just as *Coach* had

hoped, there was a slightly different mood in the group. He could tell that they were all beginning to explore this concept of the adaptation zone.

After five minutes, *Coach* stopped again. "Oh, I'm so sorry. I've just realised, I have forgotten the binoculars too. I don't suppose anyone else fancies a jog back for them?"

Should've wanted to show his disapproval. He sank to the floor and within seconds had both shoes and socks off. This was a statement of discontent.

It was clear that *Should've*'s actions were an over-dramatisation, and that instead of attracting sympathy, *Should've* was beginning to look a little silly.

Coach then remembered he had brought a small prop which he thought may come in handy to make a point and this seemed like the perfect timing.

He reached into his own backpack and pulled out a mirror and passed it to *Should've* and said firmly, "Here, look at this person, look closely. I want you to beat him not only today but every day for the rest of your life."

Should've looked down at the small mirror, then back to *Coach* and smiled. *Coach* returned the acknowledgement; he had made his point.

Could've, who had been slow to offer the last time, jumped in with, "Of course I'll go, I wanted to go the first time."

"I'll come too," volunteered *Would've*.

Coach held *Did* back and let *Could've* and *Would've* go.

"Let's chat," *Coach* continued, "did you know you have the ability to lead and inspire?"

"Not really," said *Did*, "I find the others a little frustrating, if I'm being honest. There always seems to be some doubt, an excuse or a better idea at every opportunity."

"Isn't that a very snap decision to make? After all, you've barely spent any time together and haven't really seen enough of each other's behaviour to reach such a conclusion, surely?" *Coach* remarked.

Did looked perplexed at what *Coach* had just said. He felt he was right in making such a judgement of the others.

Coach then asked, "Do you see that the others might need someone with passion, belief and clarity of purpose to lead them?"

"Probably, but that might get in the way of what I want for myself."

"You might be right, but ask yourself this — 'what can I take from my experiences with them that will help me reach my potential?'" said *Coach*.

As *Coach* stood up and started walking he said, "Maybe, they can even help you to reach your dreams."

Did couldn't see this. Surely *Coach* was the one to help him achieve that? As he was trying to decipher *Coach*'s opinion, *Could've* and *Would've* arrived back.

They walked at a strong pace up the steep, rugged terrain for a good hour and the group began to spread out – becoming fatigued. *Coach* looked back and saw that, for the first time, it was *Could've* who was beginning to struggle. He was a long way behind, with a rather despondent posture. The going was getting tough and *Could've* wasn't coping well.

Coach read *Could've*'s 'poor me' attitude and decided to push harder; he ignored his apparent cry for help as he knew going back would not be helpful for him.

He knew that any behavioural change would only come about if there was a shift in belief, and this applied to any individual. To have this shift in belief, there needed be either a huge pain or a huge gain – an experience that allowed the individual to really buy into and accept something new, not to just understand it.

Coach asked the other three to rest for a while. As they

rested, *Could've* slowly made his way towards them. As soon as *Could've* caught up, *Coach* asked them all to start again, to push on. With this, *Coach* hung back to speak to *Could've* who he could see was disappointed not to get a rest too.

"In a little over 600 days from now you could have achieved all of your current goals. But it will be the next few hundred minutes that determine if you fall into the sea of people who let yet another life–changing opportunity pass them by. The choice is yours.

"I have brought you here to test your work ethic. I don't care if your legs are tired. You are an athlete, get over it. I only work with athletes who work harder than most. You can turn around now if you wish and go back to the bottom. You can stop because it's hard. You can give in; the choice is yours. There will be many times far more difficult than this ahead, times when you will need to trust and push even harder.

"I can only guide you and hope that you see that every time you are in this adaptation zone, it is an opportunity to step closer to your dreams. This, as with everything you will do under my supervision, is your own decision. You will only achieve success by setting goal after goal after goal and by working harder. To get results you need to spend hours a day in the gym and on the track slaving your butt off, working every single muscle as hard as you can.

"Do you know what it takes to be the best you can be?"

"I'm not sure." *Could've* huffed, as he panted with fatigue.

"Well, you need to choose your goals carefully and work steadily towards them. You need to keep going until you reach them, knowing you'll be a better person for it. You need to transform your habits, your thinking, your behaviour and ultimately ... your life.

"Remember this, *success is a decision, not a gift.*" With this said, *Coach* pushed on again.

Should've hung back to talk to *Could've*, and the two spent the next hour a good way behind the others, chatting.

"What's the point in this?" whinged *Could've*. "We're sprinters, not marathon runners. I train every day, I never miss sessions, yet this crazy *Coach* thinks we should spend our time on long walks."

"I was thinking the same thing," raged *Should've*. "I have never done this sort of thing before, and I have got to where I am without it, so it can't be that important."

As the two fed each other large doses of negativity, they felt an affinity with one another. Their self–pitying mode was robbing them both of the very optimism, confidence, and growth that *Coach* wanted to instil in them.

They continued to trade negativity and stayed behind the rest of the group, out of earshot until they had offloaded all their negative points upon each other. *Could've* began to feel uncomfortable with this continuing exchange. He noticed how it was making him feel tired, heavy and drained.

"Do you think we should catch them up?" asked *Could've* in an overly casual way which belied his concern, then continued by answering his own question, "Probably should. I don't like it, but we might get lost otherwise."

The two began to close the gap between them and the rest of the group.

Coach did not look back and, despite the fact that they were now some five hours into the ascent (and he knew they'd be getting very tired), he expected them all (especially *Could've*) to be right behind him any minute.

Just as he had confidently expected, he soon heard clambering footsteps behind him and slowed to let them both pass. *Coach* was pleased, but didn't acknowledge them other than with a modest smile to himself.

The four athletes were now giving *Coach* what he wanted, they were working really hard.

A little way on, when they had been walking together as a group for a while, *Coach* asked them all to stop as he wanted to take some time to talk to them about something he felt was important.

The group stopped, dropped their packs and began to rest.

Coach said, "Based on the first of the rules I introduced, I want to hear that every individual in this group is prepared to commit to working hard. No, I mean really hard; harder than you have ever worked before."

Coach stressed that one of the key questions they should ask themselves is not "How much potential do I have?" but "How much of that potential am I currently using?"

Coach again, just like he had when he delivered the rule, stood at his full height and lifted his chin to emphasise his next point even more: "The amount of inherent potential you have is finite, but how much of that potential you exploit is completely optional."

Coach then asked them to look in their backpacks and to take out the pen and notepad he had earlier placed there. He then asked each of them to start writing their personal commitment plan.

Coach also knew that by writing this down, they were much more likely to commit to it. *Coach* explained that they had to talk about their commitment with the rest of the group and also asked them, when they got back, to e-mail their commitment plan to their three best friends and their family. *Coach* knew that by doing this he'd gain commitment from each of them, as well as acceptance and support from the people that were important to them.

Coach knew that time was of the essence, and that the level of commitment needed to be successful at this cutting edge of performance was high, so this would help to influence the amount of effort and focus each of the group would apply.

"Start doing this now while we are resting here; I would like you all to continue with this task when we get safely down to the bottom of the mountain. Is everyone okay with this?" Without waiting for their answer *Coach* continued, "I want to stress that this is not a test, it is a personal message from you to yourself.

"I want you to give it lots of thought. Maybe while you are hurting and the blisters on your feet are fresh and raw, you may see the bigger picture. This may inspire you to start to think about what really matters to you and to identify *why* you are going to commit to your dreams.

"If you would like any help, I'd be delighted to oblige. That is why I'm here."

Coach paused and made eye contact with each of his talented prodigies before him. When he was satisfied he had their full attention he continued, "I stress, this is not a test. Just be true to yourself.

"All I want you to do is to answer two simple questions. 'What do I want?' And, the most important question you can ever ask yourself, 'Why do I want it?'

"Really explore these questions; search for the most honest answers."

Coach then handed each of them a handwritten note.

Coach *Quote*

Trust in your own beliefs or succumb to the influence of others'.

Rule 2

Champions have Great Awareness

What you don't know might hurt you!

They had reached the top of the mountain in good time and now began the steep descent.

"Did you know most accidents on a mountain happen on the way down?" *Coach* asked the group. "Why do you think this might be? I'll leave that question with you for now, but it is something that I'd like you to think about as we begin our training together."

Coach was pleased, as all of the athletes had convinced him, at least verbally, of their intentions. He believed in each of their abilities and trusted that if they decided to commit, and had enough motivation and belief, then each one of them could go all the way. They were all physically good enough and *Coach* believed that any one of them was a champion in the making, if only they chose to behave effectively. This was where *Coach* felt he could affect their performance most readily.

He knew more than enough about sprinting and was confident he could deliver effective training programmes. However, *Coach* knew that it was *how* they would do the training – rather than *what* they did – that would be most important to their success.

Descending the mountain required greater concentration than the journey up had done, due to the unstable and inconsistent ground underfoot – *Coach* hoped the group were questioning why this was more hazardous.

Later, during a less steep section of the walk, *Coach* decided to share some insights from other athletes he had previously worked with. The hard work was done for the day; he had made his point, and hopefully the experience had opened their minds to the importance of wanting to work hard and retaining that work ethic.

As they took a momentary rest, *Coach* said, "I'd like to tell you about some of the other athletes I have met or worked with and what you can learn from them."

Coach knew that the first step in bringing about change was having acute awareness.

"We could spend hours discussing why it took some athletes so long to change once and for all, but the pertinent question for this chat is: did they always have the potential to create amazing change? Of course, the answer is yes.

"They didn't wake up one day and miraculously possess more potential. No, they woke up one day and started tapping into what had always been there.

"Some of these athletes didn't always have the mindset, the awareness, the discipline or the momentum – but they always had the *potential* for incredible transformation.

"For a range of reasons, there was a time when some were not ready. Not prepared to pay the price. Not willing to get that uncomfortable. Not willing to face their fears. The potential was there, but it wasn't being exploited. Just imagine owning a top of the range car but leaving it parked up because you were afraid that somebody might run into it."

Getting this across to the group would be one of *Coach*'s challenges and it was crucial for him to be aware of how they received this advice.

"I worked with this one guy," *Coach* continued, "who was, on the face of it, one of the most talented athletes I have ever known. He was on a par with each of you.

"The difficulty for him was in understanding the importance of change. What ultimately stopped him becoming a champion is that, as he progressed and changed physically, he did not adapt mentally. Little things which, compounded together, would have made this difference.

"For example, he would have stupid accidents due to not looking ahead or failing to read a situation. He did not eat well but wouldn't change his diet as he couldn't see the problem.

"He would always be late for training, but didn't see this as a problem either. He would never look at a situation and ask himself 'what would happen if ...?'

"Eventually, after many years, he began to learn what he *should* do – but it was too late. He had missed his chance."

Coach paused, and looked *Should've* directly in the eye before shifting his attention to *Would've*. He continued, "I had another guy who lacked desire. He just wasn't that into his sport. This frustrated me too!

"The most annoying thing was that he could have been great, just by having the desire to make a few small changes, but couldn't see it and therefore didn't have the desire to step up."

Finally he turned and held *Could've*'s attention. "There was one other guy who really doubted his own abilities, but this guy became strong because he listened and accepted that he could develop."

Coach paused to let the group absorb what he had just said, and then continued, "Isn't that great news? Of course, there's no way of knowing, measuring or quantifying exactly how much potential we each have – or how much of that potential we will typically use in a lifetime – but it's my belief, and my experience, that most of us don't use most of what we have.

"So, the next obvious question is: what stops us from

exploring, developing and maximising our potential?"

Could've had his hand in the air like an eager schoolboy, *Coach* was keen not to let *Could've*'s ego become deflated if he got it wrong so he quickly went on, "Well let me tell you, it's a fear thing. Fear of failure. Fear of being judged. Fear of the commitment required. Fear of the potential pain, discomfort and risk.

"The day we decide that we're prepared to deal with those inevitable realities of the human experience, and the day we stop trying to keep everybody except ourselves happy, is the day that the transformation begins.

"All I care about is what you do with what you've been given. You can't change your genetics, but you can change how you use them. You can't change your biological age, but you can change what you *do* at your age.

"Although you can't go back in time and alter your natural level of potential, you can determine how much of that ability you tap into, exploit and develop for the future.

"For many, lack of achievement is more a consequence of fear of taking a chance and getting uncomfortable.

"Many unsuccessful people allow self-limiting beliefs to stand between them and success. This often allows a divergent mind to prevail, and that doesn't give the focus required. For success in sport we need to focus with a converging thought process. All those jumbling thoughts of a divergent, deviating mind can take you away from your goal."

"Do you believe in us, *Coach*?" asked *Should've*.

"Yes, one-hundred per cent. What I'm saying is even if you're good enough, talented enough, strong and fast, you'll still need to trust in yourselves and have the desire and belief to explore your potential."

*****

They walked for the next mile or so without anyone talking. *Coach* became preoccupied with the next part of their experience.

He had led them to a very specific point and, just as he had planned, the unusual terrain where he had planned to execute the next lesson was just visible in the distance as the five of them had taken a detour off the main path.

Unbeknown to the athletes, *Coach* was leading them up to a rather precarious blind summit, beyond which was a kind of deep crevice – a sudden drop. He wanted to use this to make a point; safely, he hoped.

Coach talked about things around them to distract their attention from the series of ledges in the distance that stepped down to a ravine. *Coach* knew that while it was safe to approach, there was only one way to cross which wasn't obvious.

Coach suddenly stopped and said, in a strong voice, "Who trusts me and wants me to take them to their dream?"

All four expressed their agreement.

"Do you understand that every decision you make, every choice you make has a consequence?" asked *Coach*.

"Yeah," said *Did*, "for every action there is an equal and opposite reaction, right?"

Coach went on, "Thank you, *Did*. You will make decisions sometimes without even being aware that you are doing so. For example, you have all decided to work with me. And you have decided to follow me down this part of the mountain. That is your choice: attitude is a choice. A better attitude equals better decisions, behaviours and outcomes," finished *Coach*.

"Do you mean we all subconsciously consented to this torture?" asked *Should've*.

"Yes," replied *Coach*, "To get what you want, first you have to think about what you want and focus your attention on finding solutions – not problems. When you perform this you get your conscious mind and your subconscious mind functioning to help you get what you want – not what you don't want."

"So that's who is to blame for all of this pain today ... my subconscious mind," said *Should've*.

Coach smiled and said, "Your subconscious mind will believe whatever you tell it. By applying this method of focusing on what you want, eradicating negative thoughts, letting go and exploring new possibilities, you will get what you want.

"This is a way of telling yourself that you sign up to it ...."

"Sign up for what?" asked *Would've*.

"Hold on, let me finish," said *Coach*, "By accepting that you are prepared for the creative part of your mind to find solutions, that is your way of signing up to it."

Could've said, "But you know, *Coach*, I ask myself every day 'when am I going to be a winner?', but I never get any answers."

"The way forward is to stop pestering yourself for answers and let it, the creative part of your mind, come up with the solution when the time is right. You must begin to ask yourselves the right questions.

"When you get an urge to do something that will help you accomplish your goals, go ahead, but pay attention. Listen to what others say, listen to what others suggest, see every little thing that unfolds as an opportunity to help you achieve your goal."

Would've raised his eyebrows and asked, "You literally mean we should listen to each other in this group?"

Coach replied, "Yes. You have to know when to trust and

when to challenge. When you decide what you want, trust that you are always being guided towards it and that you will get there when you make your desire a priority."

Coach changed his whole demeanour, and his manner of speech changed to a hushed yet serious tone, drawing the attention of the group. "Remember, if you don't do anything – if you don't change the way your mind works and direct your subconscious mind to create the life you want – then everything stays the same ... nothing changes."

Should've had a puzzled look on his face; he wondered where *Coach* was going with this.

Should've's reverie was broken when *Coach* suddenly asked, "Who believes they could beat me in a race to that large rock just below the horizon over there?"

Coach pointed to a large boulder that appeared to be around 200 metres away (a distance they were all familiar with); it was straight ahead, but obscured by the low sun in the sky.

However, unbeknownst to the athletes, these series of ledges and a deep crevice made it impossible to go directly to the rock.

All four laughed at this apparently ludicrous challenge from *Coach*. "Of course we could beat you," said an over–confident *Did*, and the rest summarily agreed.

"What if I said I know, with utmost certainty, that I can beat any one of you to it, if I chose to?" *Coach* asked.

The group couldn't contain themselves and laughed again. *Coach* was in his early sixties and although he looked somewhat older, he was not a toned and finely honed athlete who could even think about sprinting against anyone of the group. Maybe he could outdo them on mountain ranges, but this challenge was a ludicrous suggestion.

Could've was beginning to lose faith in *Coach* and for a moment he had a harsh thought which he would later regret:

he felt *Coach* was a bit of a fool.

"Maybe you'd like me to prove it to you?" *Coach* asked, as if reading *Could've*'s mind.

"Go on then!" *Could've chided* with a confident, challenging tone.

Coach drew a line in the ground, signifying the start line.

"Remember, *your focus determines your reality*. I want you to remember this saying. Do you know what it means? If not, when I beat you, hopefully you will understand what it means."

The group were bamboozled by what *Coach* was saying. Maybe he really had lost it?

"Okay, on your marks …."

All four athletes put a foot to the start line, exactly as they would in training.

"Get set …."

Coach still didn't take up a starting position, which baffled the athletes as they stood, primed, ready to race.

"He has no chance," thought *Should've*.

"Go!"

The four took off and had run for about 80 metres when *Coach* fired a starting pistol into the air. The echo stopped the athletes in their tracks. But to be on the safe side *Coach* had also shouted immediately after he pulled the trigger for them to stop. It was a big risk, but a well thought out strategy that was about to pay off in big dividends for *Coach*.

Should've was in the lead: he put the brakes on as soon as he heard the shot.

They all stopped suddenly and looked behind them, but *Coach* was gone! They then walked further on and could now see why *Coach* had stopped them. As they peered over the edge they could see a short drop to a ledge below and then a void.

There was no way to cross. Immediately, they all realised that they had been tricked.

"How stupid! We all got sucker–punched!" blasted *Would've*.

Did smiled to himself, realising what *Coach*'s point was. *Could've* snapped out aloud, "That daft old fool. Why would he do that?"

Could've's voice travelled and in reply came *Coach*'s answer, "To beat you!" *Coach* was on top of the boulder the four had all been running directly to — well all except *Coach*. He had been aware of the void and had taken a route he knew was safe, one which got him to the finish point.

"I won!" *Coach* triumphantly shouted across the gap. "Why?"

"'Cos you got there first!" shouted *Would've*.

"See you all at the bottom!" hollered *Coach*.

The group were feeling quite stupid, and at this point only *Did* understood what *Coach* had done and why.

The problem now was how to get down the mountain.

"Does anyone know the way?" asked a cautious *Did*.

"How ridiculous!" *Should've* blurted out in response to *Did*'s question, feeling quite uncomfortable at the prospect of being lost.

Did had made a mental note of the direction based on the position of the sun, which was now low in the sky. "That way is west; we came from the south, so we have to go this way to get down. Follow me," he said with certainty.

Coach was unaware of this (as within an hour he was sitting in his car at the foot of the mountain), but the difficult situation had thrust *Did* into a new role, and he was doing something he had never done before – taking a wider responsibility for others.

Finally all four athletes made it safely to the bottom and joined *Coach* for the short drive back to the clubhouse.

Coach had asked the question he had asked before – and it annoyed *Could've* just as much as it had done the first time – "Why did I beat you?"

"Because you knew there was a crevice there; isn't that obvious?" said a rather deflated *Could've*.

"It was to me," chuckled *Coach* with a mile–wide grin. "Why did I beat you?"

Now *Should've* was getting angry, as was *Could've*.

"'Cos you cheated!" *Should've* said abruptly.

"Cheated; really? I said I would beat you to the rock and I did; why? Am I faster than you?" asked *Coach* with mock incredulity.

Coach clearly had a point, but most of the group didn't really know what it was. It seemed to go straight over their heads, instead of into their heads. Well all except *Did*, as *Did* knew *Coach*'s reasoning behind this.

"Have a think about it; this will form a large part of your development," instructed *Coach*.

They arrived back at the track and *Coach* left the group and headed home.

Bewildered, the four stood in the car park, still trying to decipher *Coach*'s behaviour.

"His point was that he knew something we didn't. Big deal!" seethed *Could've*.

"The point is that we were ignorant and didn't read the situation well. We applied assumptions based on what we thought we knew at the time and, under the circumstances, they were false assumptions, or something like that," said *Did*.

"But how does that apply to us? *Should've* asked, perplexed.

"No doubt we'll find out tomorrow," said *Could've*.

It excited *Coach* that he could see what he referred to as *win–wins* across the group. *Coach* knew this was a very potent tool that would nurture self−confidence and a *'we'* experience. By engaging the athletes in their own development, in turn, they could all improve as a result of the dynamic created by working together as a team.

*****

The day after the walk, the athletes arrived at the track as usual, went to the far end of the stand, and began to stretch gently as they normally would. There was, however, a different atmosphere within the group: a slight tension, a sense of frustration.

As *Coach* arrived, they acknowledged him but without much enthusiasm.

They were all tired and aching, and were still not happy about what *Coach* had done to them the previous day.

Coach understood this and tried to inject a little energy into the muted atmosphere. He asked all the athletes to meet in the clubhouse, and his tone and stature made it clear that once again he had something important to say.

Coach was keen to share his second rule and the timing seemed perfect. He needed to make sure that the group really understood this rule. It was one thing to understand the phrase, but true understanding would come from a deeper appreciation of the meaning of this − a fundamental step that would be a crucial part of the group's development.

"I hope that the experience you had on the descent was something that has initiated some thinking. While you do this I would like to share with you the second of the rules that I would like you to build into your lives. Maybe it will help you make some sense of why I did what I did."

He then shared his second rule:

RULE 2
Champions have Great Awareness

"Champions know themselves and are not afraid of being brutally honest in their self-appraisal. They have a clear and realistic understanding of their strengths, their weaknesses and also of their surroundings. In order to be a champion, you need to know exactly what the criteria are for you to perform at your best, to reach your dreams, and then need to be acutely aware of how well you are meeting these criteria as you go in search of your perfect performance."

The athletes were still smouldering inside from the race incident on the mountain when *Coach* said, in a fatherly voice, "Yesterday. Well, I should explain that I really wanted to leave you with a memory relevant to your specific skills. There's so much that you all have to go through. You see, you were so sure you would beat me, but you were not *aware*, you did not explore your territory. I mean this metaphorically, but also, in this case, literally too."

As *Coach* spoke, the group responded in kind and some of the fiery anger within them had dropped a few notches. He went on, "You can trust I always have your best interests at heart. I have your performance development in mind and, of course, your safety. If I offended you, I apologise, but it was with good intent. You see, you will remember what happened and, as a result of this shift in your awareness, if you chose to, you will change how you behave. It is an important part of your development – to improve your awareness.

"Every athlete I have met who has made it to champion

status is very aware of who they are. I have also met others who were restricted by their lack of awareness. They lacked this type of adeptness, this ability to comprehend themselves and their environment.

"The clever ones have the ability to judge, the skill to perceive and read situations that gives champions an added sharpness. This is now a trait that will grow within you all."

In *Coach*'s mind he saw beyond the overt demonstration of self–belief in *Could've* and knew that he actually suffered an inherent lack of belief when it came to it. This was the aspect that he needed to develop.

Should've, Coach realised, lacked the ability to seek out new ways of doing things. He was resistant to new ideas and made every effort to retain his current methods. It was almost like *Should've* felt that he had already found the most successful method, and if he could do the same thing over and over again, then he could expect a better result. *Coach* knew the limitations of this protective and restrictive behaviour.

Would've seemed to lack desire. Because he was a good all–rounder, he could turn his hand to many things and enjoyed the variety in doing this. *Coach* had observed that he was fairly laid–back too. It was almost like he couldn't be bothered.

Did, Coach noticed, had an insatiable desire for success and this emanated from his every pore. It seemed fairly clear to *Coach* that *Did* could benefit greatly from a team dynamic as it would stop him from over–thinking.

It also made *Coach* wonder whether it was possible to want something too much. "*Did*," *Coach* thought, "might need to just relax a little bit, trust and let things happen."

In short:

Could've still lacked belief.

Should've still lacked the ability to change.

Would've still lacked passion.

And *Did* was very focused, but *Coach* had learned that he could be accused of being insular in his outlook on training.

Coach then handed each person a handwritten note and asked them to keep it with the previous one he had given them.

Coach Quote

See it first in your mind, then become it.

Rule 3

Champions give their Dream a Higher Purpose

Your focus determines your reality

"Right, let's get going, another tough day ahead and a similar theme – low intensity, long reps. I know you all love the long stuff!" *Coach* said sarcastically, but in a light–hearted way.

Would've, who was always fairly chirpy, responded positively and started his stretching.

Could've, feeling rather grumpy, decided to express his frustration by going on the offensive. "You'll probably do the minimum as usual, won't you, *Would've*?"

"Minimum! I'm the one always out there at the front of the pack," *Would've* snapped back.

"Yeah, right. Making out that you train hard when really you're just going through the motions. You're lazy! You just fake it! When it came to pushing on and working hard yesterday, you were nowhere to be seen!"

Would've was lost for words. He wasn't used to being attacked in this way. He blushed a little and had just started to formulate a reply when *Coach* intervened.

Coach didn't like this sort of dialogue, or the atmosphere that was developing within his group, and immediately stepped in to stop it from escalating.

"*Would've*, let's walk a bit," *Coach* said.

They set out on a slow walk around the perimeter of the

track. As they walked, *Coach* began, "Don't get dragged in to *Could've*'s banter, he can be destructive at times. You know yourself how hard you are working. That's what counts.

"Try joking with him when he challenges you like that. Never show him that he has got to you," said *Coach*.

"It's not a problem. I can deal with him."

"Good," *Coach* replied, satisfied that *Would've* was sufficiently thick-skinned to cope with any further attacks.

They finished the lap. *Coach* walked over to *Could've* and asked him to join him for a walk too. They were nearly halfway round the track before *Coach* started to talk. "I worked with an athlete once, who was very talented, like *Would've*. However, he could not decide which direction to apply himself. You see, because he was well coordinated and very athletic, he could do pretty much anything he turned his hand to and he enjoyed impressing people with his range of abilities."

"Was he lazy too?" *Could've* asked in a cheeky tone.

"No. As I said, he was just like *Would've*. Not lazy, just a little lacking in direction, and therefore he didn't commit as much as he needed to ... not until he eventually found his passion and became a decathlete. This suited his physicality and his mentality; this discipline made sense to him and once he found it, he worked harder than any athlete I've ever known, including you."

"So why are you telling me this?"

"*Would've* reminds me of him. He is a good person and very talented. He just needs help in finding his passion."

"Haven't you noticed how he keeps going missing when things get tough? He makes out he is working harder than anyone but ... just watch him!" said *Could've*.

Of course, *Coach* had seen this, but he was searching for a solution and looking at the possible cause, which he read as *Would've* having not yet found his passion.

"Does it make you feel better to attack him?" asked *Coach*.

"I don't like people faking it."

"He's not; he just might need a little help to feel as fully committed as you do. Can you help him with that?"

"Why should I help him? I want to beat him," *Could've* pointed out.

"Can you see how even this annoyed feeling inside of you is in your control? It is a reaction that you have initiated. You see, the better *Would've* does, the better it is for you. You will thrive in a more positive environment. That's just how it is. Once you see that your own feelings are within your control, you can start to effect outcomes far wider than you do currently and in turn develop an even greater performance within yourself.

"Can I leave it with you to explore ways in which you develop this and to consider what you might get from a more positive environment?" asked *Coach*.

Could've gave *Coach* the minimum of acknowledgement that he would take this on. It was enough for *Coach*, though.

"Thanks, I know you will see the benefit and reap the rewards of it," *Coach* said, before walking along in silence for the remaining few yards.

They had completed the lap and returned to where the others were still stretching and joking with each other.

"What did *Coach* say?" asked *Would've*.

"He said I'm going to kick your backside in training today," *Could've* replied, before giving *Would've* a reassuring wink and heading off on his first warm-up lap.

After this pep talk from *Coach*, there was a great energy in the group.

During the training session the four athletes shared the responsibilities of leading repetitions on the track and 'spotting' for each other in the gym.

Whilst the atmosphere was competitive, it was productive, and *Coach* could see that this would be a key element in their development.

It was two years to the Olympic Games, and if any of his athletes were going to be 'on the bus' then this was a great dynamic to have, and one that would hopefully make them into champions.

Coach preferred to allow the natural dynamics of a group to flourish. He liked the organic growth that came from talented people spending time together and didn't want to be too prescriptive whilst things were working well. At the same time, his methods were challenging while giving the group the confidence they needed in themselves (and in him) through his choice of language.

Coach knew that the assumptions he had made about each of the four athletes were accurate and he really understood the consequences of the respective flaws in their behaviour.

He realised that *Could've*'s lack of self–belief would limit his ability when it came to committing to a difficult goal, such as becoming a successful athlete and competing on the world stage. He also knew that when under pressure, any lack of self–belief would be found out, as stress would really expose this aspect of *Could've*'s personality.

It wasn't yet time to take action, but when the time was right, *Coach* had a plan to help *Could've* to optimise his abilities and stand tall under pressure.

Coach knew many ways of doing this, but it was essential to get to know *Could've* a little better in order to really see how deep this lack of belief ran in him. *Coach* had learned from experience that there is always a way to tackle this issue so that *Could've*, if he chose to, would truly believe in himself. Of all the athletes' traits, *Coach* was most optimistic about turning this one around.

Coach knew that when it came to lack of self-belief, what you perceive in your own mind is more important than everything else. He said to himself, "Once you have great self–confidence and belief, you will free yourself from worries, and you will have the conviction that you can make your own life better, in both mind and body."

By looking deep down within himself, *Coach* knew that *Could've* 'could' meet every challenge that came his way with great success.

He thought to himself, "*Could've* needs to remember situations where he was not scared of failure and consider how this affected his performance."

He soon became deep in thought again ... "It is often the case that although everything around us might be going according to plan, still our feelings create discord at some level. Some sad personal history can negatively affect our growth, and the undesirable ideas in our heads can make us feel dissatisfied and lacking. Lack of self–belief will hinder our attainment of aims and objectives." This was surely the case with *Could've*.

During the afternoon gym session, *Coach* had an opportunity to talk with *Could've*, who had arrived early.

Coach asked about times when he had done well ....

"Tell me about your best ever day, *Could've*."

Could've began with a loose memory of a day when he had won a race in the past.

Coach wanted to bring their memory to life to use it as a blueprint for future success, "I want detail; I want you to re–live that memory. Where were you? Who was with you? What were you wearing? What was the weather like? How did you feel? How did you walk, think, talk to other people?" *Coach* had lots of questions and encouraged *Could've* to really try to re–live those wonderful memories.

This was a time for *Could've* to indulge himself in the positive through details in his own memories.

Could've told *Coach* about the previous year when he had competed at a small meeting at his home track. He had run a lifetime best in this competition, and won by a healthy margin in the process.

Coach wanted to know about what mind frame he was in prior to the meet and how he had managed this for himself. *Coach* really impressed upon *Could've* that he had decided to believe in himself on that day.

Yes, circumstances had encouraged him, but it was still *Could've*'s interpretation that controlled his thinking. *Coach* knew that it might take time, but if he could help *Could've* to see that he is in control, to use these past positive memories and how he felt about them, then he could start to decide a new level of self–belief. This relationship had begun well.

Coach asked *Could've*, "How often do you shower?"

Could've replied, "Oh, sorry, *Coach*! I'll make sure I shower more often."

"No, no," said *Coach*, "I simply mean, tell me how many times a week you shower?"

"Sometimes twice a day," replied a puzzled *Could've*.

"And how do you feel afterwards?"

"Refreshed."

"Good," said *Coach*. "That is how to start to become positive. You enter the shower with negative things from the day's training on you: stale sweat, micro fibres from your tracksuit, and more besides. By washing away all the negativity that surrounds you, you start to connect with yourself again, and connect with your positive thoughts, ideas and feelings. You know what, *Could've*?"

"What's that?" he replied.

"Just by thinking good thoughts may not stop your line of thinking right now, but so long as you are thinking along the lines of self-worth then you will start appreciating yourself more. Treat yourself to something special and see how good you feel within.

"Instead of letting your mind lead you to pain and suffering, why don't you take charge and consciously select what you feel and think. Just as taking a shower washes away negativity from the day's training, you can also take a 'mind shower'."

"*Coach*," said a happier *Could've*, "that sounds good to me."

Coach said, "Try to remove all of the undesirable ideas that pop up in your mind during the day, make a change and develop more optimistic and positive ideas.

"You might look at what is happening in your life and come to the conclusion that you are worthless or undeserving. At such a moment, *Could've*, think of yourself as on a level with everyone else. This means that you too have the ability to achieve and succeed, just as much as *Should've*, *Would've* and *Did*."

"When you put it that way, *Coach*, it all makes sense," said *Could've*.

"Always start with the assumption that good things will happen. If bad ideas or thoughts pop into your mind, take control of these thoughts. Whatever the picture is in your mind, reduce it in size and then move it far away, until it disappears. Bear in mind that this is a gradual process and requires great practise, but once you grasp it, you will start to realise results. Once you gain clarity and start to feel positive, you will think positively and, as a result, you will only do positive things," said *Coach*.

"As you work towards improving the direction of your thoughts and ideas, it is worth developing a more profound belief in who you are and what you are capable of.

"I'd like you to take that progression sheet that you

started on the mountain a stage further. Take the time to jot down your abilities, talents and skills. Note any good things about yourself that come to mind, no matter how trivial it seems. This self-evaluation will direct your focus towards a more positive self-awareness," said *Coach*.

"By looking back over these notes you will be able to see the bigger picture, the whole. Tracking your daily habits and progress in a journal of sorts is one way to see them realistically; it helps you to review what you have accomplished. Tracking helps to motivate you, too. If you make a change in your life and stick to it once a day until it becomes a habit, you will be more likely to keep on doing it until you progress to the next level of achievement," explained *Coach*.

Could've asked, "But how do you get into the right frame of mind to do this?"

Coach replied, "Even if you find your mood going down the emotional tube, you can raise it again. Use memories that make you feel good. Think of what made you want to become an athlete. Do things that make you feel good. Invest your energy in the things you can control."

"How can I use my notes to help me do this, *Coach*?" asked *Could've*.

"Each day, please consider whether you are serious about ditching your self–limiting beliefs. Set aside some time to look at your list and remind yourself that you can attain whatever you want, as long as you set your mind to it. Eventually, a great feeling of positivity will start to sweep over you and you will gain more self–assurance simply because you are used to being more positive. Let me have the list tomorrow morning," said *Coach*.

Coach turned his attention to *Would've*, who he hoped was beginning to understand how he needed to take control of his desire, his mood and his drive to succeed. Coach probably felt most frustrated with his type: those with bags of talent but without the level of hunger to capitalise on their abilities.

He had talked with many who were similar to *Would've* and, after their sports careers were over, all had used the 'R' word. This was a word that *Coach* hated – *regret*. This, he thought, was the biggest failing in anyone with a talent that they didn't nurture. *Coach*'s mission here was to look to develop this passion so that *Would've* might never even think about using the 'R' word.

Coach knew that in order for *Would've* to explore his full potential he would have to integrate both action and motivation, and he caught himself saying, "It's obvious, right?"

Coach was giving himself a pep talk, running 'what ifs?' through his head. "If you decide not to take action, you are going to fail, and even if you do take action, if you can't keep up your motivation, you will simply end up back where you started."

Coach recognised that most failed athletes kept going round and round in circles when trying to set goals, only to fall flat on their faces by making the same mistakes. In turn, this becomes counterproductive to their ability to get motivated in the first place. This is when an athlete feels as if everything is stacked against them. Then it just gets harder and harder to pick up their broken dreams and put them back together again. This is exactly what he didn't want to happen to *Would've*.

Coach knew what it was like to have your dreams disappear before your very eyes. He recalled the confusion he felt after his own athletics career was cut short following his accident. *Coach* thought to himself, "The world has plenty of misery stories of people with broken dreams. *Would've* isn't going to be one of them – I will make sure of that."

The evening session was over, *Coach* was happy with the atmosphere within the group. They gathered up their kit and started to leave, but *Coach* called them back for a few parting words of wisdom.

Coach noticed *Would've* was missing and asked the others where he was. Then he remembered: *Would've* had asked to leave early as he had said that he was going to a football trial – as a scout had seen his pace and told him he was good enough to be playing for the local side and that he should try out for the club. *Would've* didn't see any harm in missing part of the training session.

Coach left training that evening with a deep feeling of frustration. Yes, he could have said *no* to *Would've*'s request to leave training early, but that was not what *Coach* was about. Rather than rule with a rod of iron, *Coach* preferred to empower those he worked with. That way *Would've* was not in a position to hold anyone but himself responsible for his own actions.

He could see the potential in *Would've* and, as his coach, wanted to tap into it. This wasn't only about *Would've*'s physical ability; this was in some ways the easy bit. It was about the way he chose to apply himself.

The following day *Coach* arrived at the track ahead of the athletes. When the athletes arrived they knew something was up.

They wondered what might be coming as they were ushered silently into a quiet part of the clubhouse.

Coach began to talk, very calmly and with a great, but empowering, authority as he introduced the third rule:

RULE 3
Champions give their Dream a Higher Purpose

"Life will throw many opportunities at you, and you need to retain the passion for what it is you really, really want.

"One of the biggest challenges you will face is 'choice and distraction'. Many athletes don't get to where they want to be because they lose their way, due to 'alternatives' — things that 'distract' them along the way. Athletes who are able to stay completely focused in pursuit of their dreams are the ones that are most likely to become champions."

This rule was probably most relevant to *Would've*. Arguably, he was the most talented member of the group, but he 'would' never be the one who optimised his potential if he wasn't able to understand this crucial rule at a deeper level.

Coach waited for the athletes to go out to the track, then asked *Would've* to stay behind to discuss his interpretation of it, as *Coach* could sense a new dawning within *Would've*.

"Does this rule make sense to you?" asked *Coach*.

"It does now that you have spelled it out. I think I just needed to hear it in simple terms."

Coach knew that sometimes all it needed was a turn of the key that was already in the lock, and although admittedly this was not a foolproof way of working, it did, at times, pay off big dividends if the key that was already in the lock, had just the right amount of leverage to turn it. In this case, something just clicked and it worked, which was of no surprise to *Coach*, as he had seen this happen a number of times before in some of his champions.

"Great. I look forward to exploring that with you as you progress," *Coach* replied and then when he was out of sight of *Would've* he smiled and said to himself, "*Yes.*"

Training that evening went well, and *Coach* was proud that each athlete had really focused and given his all. The session had been particularly tough, and all four had explored their own boundaries. It seemed that they had all stepped up because of this vital understanding of giving dreams a higher purpose.

"What do you think is beyond the maximum?" *Did* asked *Coach* as they got ready to leave.

"Shouldn't the question be, 'What *is* your maximum?'?" *Coach* replied. He often gave what seemed like indirect answers.

Coach finished his point off with, "Continue to give your dream a higher purpose and you will begin to explore your true potential. Believe me when I say that there is a vast expanse beyond what you currently perceive to be your maximum."

At the end of that day's training session, *Coach* again handed a handwritten quote to each of the four, which he again asked them to keep with the quotes he had previously given them.

COACH QUOTE

Success is a decision, not a gift.

RULE 4

Champions have PRIDE – Personal Responsibility in Delivering Excellence

If not you, who?

Following the previous evening's training session *Did* had been the last to leave and he had chatted with *Coach* as he walked up the steep steps to the gate.

"Go on, run along and get some good food down you, you've worked hard today," *Coach* had said.

"I can help you lock up. Honest, it's fine," replied *Did*.

"I'd rather you stay warm and re–fuel. Now, run along!" *Coach* said in a firm but friendly way.

Did ran on, leaving *Coach* to lock up. *Coach* stopped, looked back at the track and remembered the hard work they had done that day.

Being the conscientious person he was, he noticed some litter on the steps, bent over to pick it up and slipped and fell down the stone steps. As the sun dropped out of sight for the night, *Coach* lay still: unseen and unconscious.

*****

The following morning the group arrived at the track for training and were looking forward to the session that *Coach* had prepared for them. He'd mentioned that they would be doing some speed work against the clock. The whole group loved this kind of work as it was a chance to see the fruits of their labour.

Coach was always at the track in good time, but today, for the first time, he was late. The group wondered whether they should push on with their warm–up, but were in full expectation that *Coach* was about to arrive.

"Come on, let's get on with it!" an impatient *Did* shouted as he began his jog around the track to warm up.

The first to follow was *Would've*: he didn't want the session to run late, but, more importantly, he didn't want to be left with *Should've*, who he regarded as being a bit odd. *Should've* was the most resistant to any kind of innovation but reluctantly sloped along at the back anyway.

"He's probably just stuck in traffic," *Should've* said to the others – mainly just to let them know he was now jogging along behind them.

"He's probably given up with you because of your stubborn attitude," said *Could've* over his shoulder.

As they were completing their first lap, they were stopped by one of the other coaches.

"There has been an accident; *Coach* has been taken to hospital. It looks like he fell down those steps, banged his head and lay unconscious until the police found him. His family raised the alarm, they were frantic with worry when he didn't return home and no one could reach him on his phone," he said.

"Is he okay?" asked *Would've*, visibly shaken.

"He should be, they are still uncertain though."

"Where is he? Can we go to see him?"

"He's at the General. I don't know much myself, I just thought I should let you know."

*****

Although *Coach* had been knocked unconscious, the diagnostic scan had shown that fortunately he was only suffering from a non-complex concussion and mild hypothermia.

As he lay in the hospital bed, *Coach* drifted in and out of consciousness, and in this state he was quite susceptible to his subconscious fears being unlocked.

As he drifted off into a dreamy state his mind was still working on fulfilling his own wishes ....

Coach thought to himself, "Negative thoughts are weeds in the garden of your mind."

Just then a crashing sound came from the roof of the clubhouse. "What the ...." *Coach* heard himself say out aloud.

Coach's dream became more bizarre as *Could've* shouted, "*Coach*, it's one of those destructive, negative thoughts you were telling us about ... what should we do?"

"One of you is having an attack of self–destructive thoughts. Negative thoughts can and will destroy your life! Don't you know that? A mind filled with negative thoughts makes you feel miserable and inadequate and will lead to failure after failure no matter how hard you try to succeed," shouted *Coach* anxiously.

Coach knew that one of the four had unlocked the door to negativity and it was this negative thinking that had caused what was happening around them.

"Can't you see what someone's destructive thoughts are doing; they are bringing the clubhouse down around us. Quick, we have to get out or we'll all be crushed!" yelled *Coach*.

Suddenly, and with some urgency, *Could've* said, "If you want to succeed, you have to eliminate any consistently negative thinking and negative beliefs."

Coach was shocked by this positive outlook from the usually negative thinking *Could've* and, momentarily, the building stopped crumbling around them.

"That's it," said *Coach*, excited at coming up with the

answer, "we all have to make a positive statement to balance the negativity. You have to replace those negative thoughts with positive thoughts and then you can go on to succeed and enjoy life."

But *Should've* saw things more deeply and in a flash he was saying, "Look, as much as you try you won't be able to eliminate all of your negative thinking. I mean, how can we eliminate those chronic, deep–seated negative thoughts and change the negative beliefs that prevent us from succeeding and achieving our goals?"

Coach fell deeper into this unusual dream ... the building started to fall apart around them again. *Would've*, *Should've* and *Did* made a dash for safety.

Coach said to *Could've*, "Run ... save yourself."

"No, *Coach*! I'm not leaving you with all of this negativity! I know now that negative thoughts and beliefs develop over time. They can't just come crashing down on you like this building. It's all an illusion."

"That's right," said a relieved *Coach*, "they come from your friends, your family, co–workers, advisers, teachers, even strangers – and they come from you – that's right! YOU."

"ME?" shouted an incredulous *Could've*.

"Yes, it's you that has caused this attack of negativity! Sometimes doubt sets in when you start to lose focus. If you don't know how to control your thoughts they can bring everything crashing down around you!"

Just then a concrete beam above them was beginning to come loose and was looming threateningly overhead.

"Don't you know," *Coach* said to *Could've*, "you often create most of the negative thoughts that you have, and it's because you haven't trained your mind to be positive, you haven't created positive beliefs that allow you to succeed?

"Every day you're bombarded with a series of negative

thoughts, negative messages and as you continue to absorb all of these negative messages you create destructive thinking patterns, just like you are doing now."

Suddenly, some masonry plummeted down and trapped one of *Coach*'s legs. Although not crushed, his leg was firmly wedged.

"Save yourself! Leave me," *Coach* said to *Could've*. "These negative thoughts are too powerful; they are destroying all of your positive thoughts and beliefs. These are the type of thoughts that don't allow you to succeed and will only lead to more failure."

"*Coach*, tell me how to get rid of these destructive thoughts ... quick," shouted *Could've*.

The concrete beam above them broke loose from one of its mountings, swinging wildly and missing *Coach*'s head by centimetres, leaving a trail of dust over both *Coach* and *Could've*. The air was now filled with acrid smoke from an electrical fire which had broken out.

As the dream continued, *Coach* explained to *Could've* how to rid himself of the negative thoughts that were causing this chaos. "You start by replacing them with positive thoughts and positive feelings. When you have a negative thought that says you can't do something, then you think of the reasons why you *can* do it. Change those negative thoughts and think about what can go right. Just think of how you accomplish anything you put your mind to. Recite affirmations; this is your new, positive way of thinking. You have to continue to foster positive thoughts in your mind."

"If I do that, *Coach*, how soon will I start to see changes?" asked *Could've,* frantically looking up at the beam that was about to crash down on *Coach*.

"You will start to see changes when that sort of positive thinking becomes a reflex habit to anything that is even remotely connected to negative thoughts," coughed *Coach* through the billowing smoke, "when you eliminate the destructive, negative thinking then you will see change."

Could've began to do as *Coach* said, and started to empower himself with positive thoughts and beliefs: "I am ready to accept positive thoughts and change."

As *Could've* kept repeating this phrase, *Did* had come back into the wrecked building, he grasped *Coach* under his arms, and, with all of the strength he could muster, he gave a mighty heave and pulled *Coach* free – seconds before the beam overhead crashed loose from its final mounting bolt.

The sound of the crashing beam jolted *Coach* out his anxiety–ridden dream, but soon he returned to a deep, healing sleep.

*****

Back at the track *Did* asked the others, "Do you think we should finish the session?"

"How can we? *Coach* is lying in hospital and you are worried about your training," said *Should've* in an agitated, raised voice.

"He would want us to. Let's do the session, then all go to visit him together," suggested *Did*.

The group went through the session just as *Coach* had prescribed and then went to the hospital.

In the waiting area the athletes talked about whether they could have prevented the accident.

"It's my fault. I should have waited and helped *Coach* lock up. We should have looked out for him," said a guilt–ridden *Did*.

"It's not your fault. It's not anybody's fault. Accidents happen, it's just one of those things," *Could've* said with understanding.

84

The group were taken to a private room and a doctor explained, "You can see him briefly; he has been drifting in and out of consciousness all day. He's going to be okay, but he needs plenty ...."

Before the doctor could finish, *Would've* found himself angry that the doctor was simply referring to *Coach* as 'he', so interrupted, "*Coach* ... err, he's *Coach*."

"Well," the doctor continued, "*Coach* has some head injuries; he is in a stable but serious condition. You can go in now but please, no surprises."

The four entered the room and gathered in awkward silence around the bed.

Coach's eyes momentarily opened and he returned to consciousness. Recalling his dream, he whispered, "Ah, I see you all made it to safety, then?"

Did asked, "What do you mean, *Coach*? Safety?"

"Well, I've just had an amazing dream about something that we each have to face up to. It was a dream about something that we all hope will never happen ... it was about confronting our fears."

"Ah, I see. I thought that bang to your head had done some serious damage," said a relieved *Did*.

"Anyway, how was the training session? You all completed it?" *Coach* enquired.

"Forget the session, *Coach*. We all feel awful that we left you at the track and that this happened. I should have stayed with you." *Did* was regretful as *Coach* described how he recalled slipping on the steps after trying to pick some litter up and how, hours later, he was found at the bottom of the steps by the police when his family couldn't contact him.

"Well, in that incredible dream I had, you saved me, *Did*. It wasn't your fault; sometimes bad things just happen." *Coach* managed a weary chuckle and a thought flashed through his sore head: the dream he had just had was actually about his own fears. This was *Coach*'s subconscious mind working out how to instil positivity into the four.

The fears within *Coach*'s own mind had momentarily taken hold during his unconscious sojourn, but that was all it was ... a dream. Now *Coach* crushed those negative thoughts just as he had taught *Could've* to in the dream.

Coach thought of his family, who had rushed to see him in the early hours of the morning, exchanging words of comfort and relief.

After realising how worried they had all been, and seeing the scared look on their faces before they realised he wasn't as critically injured as they had feared, he was determined to do things differently.

He recalled how he had never been able to spend quality time with his children when they were younger as he was always working away or working late, even at weekends – his choice of lifestyle. He had dedicated his life to coaching. His son was now in a career, a public relations professional. His daughter had married into nobility, her future assured.

Yes, *Coach* was looking forward to spending time with his family, and since this was his swan song he was going to fulfil his own dream and not retire with the 'R' word. If this had of happened earlier in his career then he would have not had a second thought about calling it a day, but he knew he had the chance of maybe even putting together four athletes of supreme ability in a sprint relay team to compete at the Olympic Games.

After his car accident he had said to his wife that he was going to take up teaching, but it was at her insistence and with her blessing that he continued in some capacity in the field of athletics. Because of his active mind she knew he might grow bored, and, after all, she wanted the best for her husband.

This wasn't just *Coach*'s swan song, it was also out of

respect to all of those times his wife and then his son and daughter had supported him during his coaching career. He also owed it to them to reward their belief in him with this success, and it would make his career all the more worthwhile and his retirement a one without the 'R' word in it.

Coach mustered his strength and said to the four, "Forget what happened, you could not have changed this. This is not something you could have influenced. I need you to see this and notice the difference between things that concern you and things you can actually change. Now, I want you all to think about the recent competition. I want you all to think about what you learned, what you would do differently if you were given another chance. What *is* and what is *not* under your control? Sometimes, this is not clear and is something you need to decide."

Did was still left with the feeling that this accident was something that *could* have been under his control. He felt frustrated and confused as to what *was* and what *was not* his responsibility. Clearly, this was something that he needed to explore, as it was about optimising performance.

The group left *Coach*'s room at the doctor's request, but had been told that they could wait if they wanted to.

They decided to wait.

*****

Should've spoke in a reflective, emotional tone, "He has taught me lots already."

"He's going to be alright, he's just banged his head. Don't go getting all 'emotional' on us," *Could've* challenged, rather predictably.

Should've continued, "He's taught me so much in such a short time, starting with the power of working hard; I get that now. He's also taught me about giving my dream a higher purpose, I get that now too. He's shown me the power in having clarity.

"But do you know what? I kind of knew these things already, but I just didn't know how to apply myself in a way that really made them happen.

"By far, the biggest lesson I have learned is around this concept of awareness. You see, without awareness I would not have recognised that I was deficient in the other rules he has taught us.

"I have developed from being an athlete who was ignorant to one that now understands my weaknesses, albeit I have to start working on them. I now know that I need to do something about them. That is such a great gift and I feel completely indebted to *Coach*."

"He has taught us all an immense amount already," *Would've* agreed. "I have 'drifted' for many years, but I am beginning to feel more inspired, more motivated. He has had that effect on me.

"I have always been resistant to new ideas, to any kind of change in my life. But now find myself asking 'what if …?' He gave me that."

"No one gave you that, you've always had it, but you've only just decided to start accessing it," *Did* said.

"You're beginning to sound like him," *Could've* said.

Should've saw the relevance of this and how *Did*, indeed, was starting to sound more and more like *Coach* every day. Upon seeing this, *Should've* for the first time in his life, began to feel inspired to change.

The following day the group were handed a note that that had been written by *Coach*. *Did* took control and read it out:

RULE 4
Champions have PRIDE – Personal Responsibility in Delivering Excellence

"Champions decide to be accountable for each aspect within their control. There is never blame for mistakes, just a way of learning from an experience. You will see that the worst thing to do is to make no decision, and that learning from error is part of being a champion. Every time a champion makes a decision they have a chance to learn something new, regardless of the outcome.

"Champions take responsibility for their performance and understand consequence."

The next few weeks passed with *Coach* recovering and the group beginning to take responsibility for their own work in their training sessions. As they became increasingly aware of their responsibility towards simple things like being ready for training, arriving on time, understanding what was needed for the session and how they would feel during and after each training hour that passed, each athlete began to really understand that more of their performance was under their control than they had each thought possible.

Could've realised that his beliefs were within his control.

Should've realised that it was his responsibility to instigate change.

Would've started to understand that it was his responsibility to develop increased passion for his sport.

Did was really growing from the dynamic of working as part of a group and was enjoying the unexpected benefits of helping others out.

The most exciting aspect of this rule is that, due to the circumstances which prevented *Coach* from attending training, the group were beginning to take responsibility for each other's performance, how they felt and how they could assist each other.

Coach received numerous updates from the athletes.

"I could not have planned this any better if I'd tried," he thought to himself, and then wrote another note, ready to give each of the group when he was back in shape.

Coach Quote

If not you, who? If not now, when?

RULE 5

Champions have Clarity of Vision and a Clear Purpose

Clarity affords focus

The general mood in the group was competitive with good–natured, light–hearted banter each day as the four went about their routines with real commitment. *Coach*, now back from his short spell in hospital, was his old self again and he liked what he saw.

The first thing he did when he returned was to gather all the athletes around him to clear the air of any negativity that might be hanging around since he had been away, although this was as much to clear *Coach*'s head as the athletes' heads.

"I'd like you to consider that there are only two kinds of people in this world – those that want to drain the energy out of you, and those that give energy to you. You'll be able to tell those that are giving you energy: they're enthusiastic and positive; they leave you feeling energised and elated.

"Then there are the energy sappers.

Looking at *Could've*: "They can lack self–belief."

He shifted his gaze to *Should've*: "They also usually hate change."

He then looked at *Would've* and continued: "At times they lack passion."

Finally, he looked directly at *Did*: "They can be just too single–minded."

could've   should've   would've   did

You could have cut the tension in the air with a knife. *Coach* was back with a vengeance!

He continued, "The energy sappers are always complaining, always moaning, and they can leave you feeling exhausted and irritable. Avoid these sorts at all costs."

Well, if *Coach* had meant that literally, it would mean the four would have to avoid each other. But *Coach* always had method in what some perceived to be his madness.

"Goals," *Coach* said, "are not for dreamers. To think is good. To obsess is bad. Who here is still struggling with the idea of manifesting success to maximise their goal of winning?" Without waiting for an answer *Coach* carried on talking, "To some, realising your life's dreams and goals and applying focused, positive thoughts to your day can seem like a real struggle."

The athletes each gave one another a knowing look that meant they were all in agreement with what *Coach* was saying to them.

"You're trying so hard to get it right that you can sometimes feel annoyed and intolerant of those around you, especially when you aren't getting the results you want. That's the first problem!" said *Coach* with a passion.

"You can say that again, *Coach*," said *Did*.

Coach continued, "Those people will tell you that your

dreams are impossible, and they will try to dissuade you from believing in yourself and pursuing your goals.

"Until you reach the point in your self–development, where you no longer allow people to affect you with their negativity, you need to avoid these energy sappers at all costs!"

"How do you do that, *Coach*?" asked *Should've*.

"How do you do that? *Coach* repeated. "You have to make a conscious decision to surround yourself with positive, uplifting people. These are the people who will encourage you to go after your dreams and will inspire you to succeed. Stick to them like a barnacle to a rock. That's how you do that, *Should've*.

"In turn, others will pick up on your new, positive outlook. No matter what your height, if you think tall then you will walk tall.

"If you have positive energy you will always attract positive outcomes. In the end you'll attract what equates to your energy. If you want this to happen then it will. Change your energy to pep and vigour and you'll start to get what you want."

"What about our belief system, how does it come into this?" asked *Would've*.

They were all ears as *Coach* replied, "Your unconscious mind picks up on your feelings and your thinking; it creates situations that correspond to your thoughts and beliefs. When you think a positive thought, you become positive."

"That's what I want," said an excited *Did*.

"Well, *Did*," said *Coach*, "When your competitors sense this winning aura around you then even though they're not knowingly aware of your energy, you can be sure that they already know that you are going to be tough to beat."

Did was completely absorbed by what *Coach* had said to him. He was beginning to understand what it would feel like being really focused and what *Coach* might call being 'in the zone'.

Coach said, "Success is virulent. Once you get the bug then it's in you.

"The people and successes in your life mirror your beliefs. By changing the way you see things, you start doing away with negative thoughts and negative beliefs."

Did asked, "What about all this pent up emotion within us, you know when we get touchy at the merest of things, silly things?"

"Look for solutions, instead of being difficult; be more thoughtful, instead of allowing anger to burn you out. Look at things from a different perspective, embrace change, look out for opportunities and you will feel much more in control.

"When you are more positive, you stand a better chance of achieving your goals and are more likely to enjoy winning," *Coach* replied.

Coach finished his discourse with a little food for thought, "Tell me your thinking, and I'll tell you what your life looks like.

"Right, who's for a time trial?"

*****

At the end of the morning session, *Coach* sat with *Would've* and asked him about his dreams, what was important to him, and encouraged him to look forward and envisage the route he could see most clearly and which he trusted would unfold into reality.

Would've opened up to *Coach*: "I have often felt compromised by how and what I should do next in my life. I often find it very difficult to make decisions and then, even when I do finally decide upon something, I wonder if I have made the right decision. Maybe I'm just not as driven as some people."

"Maybe you haven't decided on your chosen journey yet?"

Coach thought about how each of us makes hundreds of decisions on an unconscious level each day, and this was reflected in what he said next: "You have many decisions to make and many more crossroads in your life. This is a wonderful position to be in. The challenge for you is to decide not what is important, but what is *most* important and then focus your attention on that.

"If you spread yourself too thinly, you will be a very talented all–rounder. There is no shame in this. Multi–eventers are often considered the most talented athletes in the world. All I ask is that you make this decision based on your own preferences rather than being led by others or by circumstances. Once you commit, do it with all of your heart. If you do this, you will find more passion than you ever knew you had. Your current apathy is simply your soul telling you that it is confused. I suggest you give it some direction."

When *Would've* returned for the afternoon session *Coach* was keen to chat to him about his foray into becoming a football player. *Coach* was supportive of *Would've*, but at the same time he wanted to challenge him about what he really wanted. He chose to do this in a light–hearted way. He wanted *Would've* to think for himself.

Coach knew it would be wrong to dictate his thoughts to *Would've*. Everything that *Coach* believed in was based on encouraging his students to make their own decisions and coming up with their own commitment plan. He hoped that *Would've* could see the opportunities before him, both as an athlete and also as a footballer.

Coach had to wait to see where *Would've*'s heart would take him – football or athletics. The difficulty *Coach* had was that whilst he wanted to keep *Would've* on the training team, he had to have complete commitment from him and this might take time.

Coach wanted *Would've* to commit despite the bumpy road ahead, the hard work and the 'risk' in not getting what he wanted, and to understand that nothing was guaranteed. This would demonstrate a true passion. He also wanted him to make this decision with no regrets.

Coach said to *Would've*, "I wonder, are your beliefs aligned to your goals in life? I mean, are you ready to attract what you really want? Sometimes it's not what you do that counts, but what you *don't* do. Neglecting your training, for example, or ignoring your dreams.

"When you find out where your talents lie, then that is when you can ultimately change your life, but not before. You have to ask yourself this, 'What is the most transformative experience I can engage in to finally achieve my greatest goals and dreams?'."

Coach encouraged *Would've* to explore so that he knew what he was buying in to. He didn't want to see *Would've* eventually retire with the 'R' word on his mind.

Coach then asked *Would've* to make his choice between the two sports. He gave him time but said, for the sake of the group, he would need to know as soon as possible what he had decided to do, as any delay could destabilise the group dynamic.

A good few weeks passed and *Coach* was delighted when *Would've* approached him after a training session at the track

"I want stay in the group. My dream is to compete at the Olympic Games and I want to see this through. This is what I want with my head and my heart."

Coach was pleased, for *Would've* and for the rest of the group.

"You know, *Would've*, you have dispelled the myth that

people with a positive mental attitude are 'cheesy'. Truly positive people do not expect perfection, but, to a certain extent, they expect that every event is the best thing that could have happened in that second."

Coach smiled at *Would've* and then he turned and looked at the other three and asked, "Do you want to know what one of the secrets to achieving all of your goals is? You've got to be committed. You've got to *want* to succeed and not let anything stop you. You've got to be able to taste success and see yourself on the winners' rostrum. You've got to give your ideas power. Go beyond the horizon. You need to have a burning desire! So, tell me this, who here has a burning desire?"

Knowing that *Coach* never usually stopped for an answer, no one answered.

This, however, was not one of those moments where *Coach* 'pushed' on. He wanted an answer, and he waited, but was met by silence. He broke it with a loud but generous helping of joviality: "WHO?" and they all laughed at *Coach*'s over–dramatised tone, including *Coach*.

Things were settled back into a routine since *Coach*'s return from his little accident. The group were all progressing very well and *Coach* was not only pleased about this but also by the fact that they were all starting to behave, in some small ways, like champions.

Did seemed to be the one who was at the back of the group for most of the sessions. He would always give his all but the other three just had the edge on him.

One evening, after one of these tough sessions where *Could've* (despite the fact that he lacked belief), *Should've* (despite the fact that he hated change), and *Would've* (despite the fact that he had little passion) had all beaten him, *Did* was feeling particularly motivated and driven.

Could've, as was often the case, decided to challenge

Did. "Do you think you've got what it takes, *Did*?" he asked.

After a long pause *Did* replied, "... I don't know. I come here day in, day out and see three other guys more talented than me, but somehow, after every session, I feel more driven towards my dream."

"What's that then?" *Could've* asked in a nonplussed tone.

"To be the best I can possibly be is the simple answer. I would love to compete at the Olympic Games. I can see myself standing over my starting blocks, looking down the track, and sometimes I even allow myself to picture standing on the winner's rostrum. I'm prepared to do whatever it takes to get there. You see, when I was a kid I was different to most. I would watch the Games on the TV and dream it was me. I would imagine what it would feel like to have that kind of experience.

"When I see myself standing on an Olympic rostrum, I begin to wonder how great that might feel; it sends a tingle of excitement down my spine when I allow myself to create that image in my mind.

"Every day I tell myself that I can do this, and that builds my confidence. I realise that I must continually search for new and better ways. I dare to dream, and follow these dreams: this gives me passion. And this is why I believe that very slowly, I am catching you all up. Every time that you all beat me it fills me with determination, with an even greater hunger to improve.

"I believe I am realistic, and I realise that there are many lessons to learn and much work to be done, but I do believe with all my heart that, that I am destined to have that experience; it's as if it is 'meant to be'."

Did had spoken with such passion and determination that the group fell silent for a good few seconds, and then *Could've* piped up with, "You must be looking forward to meeting Father Christmas too!"

"I know you doubt me," *Did* said, "I know you doubt yourself: that is your challenge and I wish you well. I am not saying this in an arrogant way, I'm just telling you of my dream. I am not looking for your blessing, or for any kind of acknowledgement. I am simply sharing my passion with you as I feel we are getting to know each other better."

"And how do you know you can do this?" asked *Should've*.

"I don't, but I'm prepared to commit one–hundred per cent to finding out and I won't give up until I know I have given my all. I am prepared to reach the pinnacle of my career by giving it my best shot," *Did* replied.

Coach was just out of earshot, but he had understood the gist of the conversation and was pleased that *Did* had shared his thoughts and feelings with the group.

"If only they could become more like him," he thought to himself.

The one athlete that *Coach* never had to worry about was *Did*. *Coach* thought he should pay more attention to him and ensure that what he had assumed was what *Did* also felt. *Coach* moved to join his number one prodigy and asked *Did* about his training, his dreams and if he had any frustrations within the group.

After speaking of his dreams, *Did* was able to open up more. He explained to *Coach* that he had something on his mind that was bothering him: he often grew frustrated by some of the others in the group who didn't focus during training.

Did explained how he had been particularly annoyed at *Would've* one evening and had snapped at him. *Coach* remembered this and had let it pass at the time, but was now annoyed that he hadn't dealt with it there and then.

Coach asked *Did*, "Do you know what makes a champion? Drive, not giving up. You are cultivating your burning desire; when you pay attention to others, you can lose focus. Remember what I said about energy sappers?"

"I get that bit, *Coach,* about the energy sappers, but the bit I don't get is the difference between being focused and being selfish," *Did* remarked.

Coach explained, "Focus retains awareness of what is around you, it is about dedicating yourself to a predetermined outcome. This is not selfish, this is behaving like a champion. Some athletes don't dedicate themselves consistently and instead make every decision on things that are important to them only from their perspective – this is self–centred and selfish. Champions stay focused, by being driven and consistent to their dreams, whilst respectful to others around them."

"Will this guarantee success?" asked *Did*

"Securing great or even Olympic success ultimately begins with an idea," Coach said, "but what makes an idea become reality is how much you really want it, how much you stay focused on it and retain that focus and intention.

"Imagining becoming a champion is only a temporary feeling. To *become* a champion is to become a permanent inspiration others look to. It is the desire to become a champion that steers and navigates you past the obstacles along the way. If those obstacles are large, jump higher. Reach for the stars.

"Make some notes about how committed you are to achieving your goals, and give them to me tomorrow morning."

"*Coach*, do you ever read these notes?" asked *Did* in a quizzical sort of way.

Coach said, "You can give me that questioning look, like you think you know what's going on, but tell me, *Did*: do you *hope* to become a champion, or do you *know* you will become a champion?"

Did had a steely look in his eyes. "I *will* become a champion. If you want something badly enough, then you pay the price, whatever it takes."

Coach said, "Well that answers your question then. Do you think if what you wrote down meant nothing to me that I would keep asking you to write your thoughts? Of course not.

"I know from reading your notes that being intensely driven in your desires is reserved for the special few. You ask yourself in your notes if this special quality is reserved for you, right?"

Did knew that he had written this fear down in some of the past notes he had given *Coach*, and now he felt bad at having questioned the integrity of *Coach* and before he could answer....

"Time will tell; however, with the right approach, anyone can grow this deep, burning desire within themselves, move to a state of total dedication and be confident that success is as predictable as the sunrise," said *Coach*.

"How do I create such a burning desire and then how do I keep the flame of that burning desire alive?" asked *Did*.

Coach replied, "You begin with an external approach by looking at what is around you and affecting it so that it sits in your favour. Know what may assist you on your journey and make sure everything around you is contributing positively to take you where you want to go. I'm talking about everything from who you spend time with, to where you live, what facilities you have at your disposal and all the routines you have inside and outside of your training time, from how you travel, what you eat and sleep – everything.

"There will also be times when you need to know how to adapt, internally. You will need to become chameleon–like sometimes in your approach. You will alter your state to suit your environment.

"If you take the time to do both of these approaches effectively, you'll set up a positive response sequence within yourself, such that your aspiration will increase on a daily basis. You will feel like you can deal with any eventuality."

*****

The athletes trained hard through the winter and continued to progress well through the long, dark, gruelling months. *Coach* continued to challenge, support and encourage his group to deliver consistent and high quality routines, week in week out as the winter progressed. He knew the importance of repetition being the most important thing that any athlete would need to help develop a robust and comfortable performance. *Coach* believed in doing the basics well. This wasn't the time for any complicated training, it was time to do the necessary donkey work to build a great speed, power and coordination. The group worked hard every day and all were slowly progressing physically, tapping into their potential, nurturing their talent and growing.

Spring soon came, and it was time to compete in an early–season race, to get back into competition mode and to assess how far they had all come. *Coach* had chosen a local, low–key event for this.

The four athletes travelled with *Coach* in his car to the meeting, at which while being low–key, there was an air of tension, typical for the first run–out of the new season – there were a lot of unknowns.

It was time for *Could've* to challenge his self–belief, *Should've* to explore the changes he'd made, *Would've* to demonstrate some passion and for *Did* to see how much he could gain on the others from delivering effectively.

The group arrived at the track in what they thought was

good time, but the race time was changed at the last minute. This presented a huge difficulty to *Should've* due to his lack of flexibility to change. In short, *Should've* wasn't able to adapt his pre–race routine. He was only halfway through his preparation when the officials called the athletes to the call room. This upset *Should've*: he reacted poorly, arguing with an official that he needed more time. *Should've* then raced in a negative frame of mind and, as a result, he under–performed.

Coach knew *Should've* well and realised that it was simply his lack of ability to adapt that had been his downfall.

"I'm not going to pull any punches with this one," said *Coach*. "What is more important, being right or being successful? If your goals are truly important to you then you have to learn to notice what is around you and adapt accordingly. You did not do this today."

Coach was going to have to invest some extra time in *Should've*. He knew that he had the potential to be a champion.

They sat and chatted, and, as ever, *Coach* wrote notes in his diary. He tore a page he'd written on, folded it half and handed it to *Should've*.

"*Coach*, what did you just write?"

"Open it."

At the top of the page it read:

It's time to say goodbye to all of these bad memories, to explore new ideas and to embrace change.

Coach then altered his stature, as he usually did when he was going to say something of a powerful consequence, and said, "Not just those bad memories, *Should've*, but it's also time to let go of the negative thoughts from today that will prevent you from achieving success tomorrow.

"Many people hang on to things that have, at some point, hurt or angered them. In fact, some don't just hang on to them, they nurse them, they keep thinking about them."

Should've thought to himself and replied, "Yeah, I know what you mean, *Coach*."

"These feelings will eventually destroy your chance of success. By hanging on to them you can't move forward, can't grow or achieve success. Hanging on to what has been will destroy your future."

With a despondent note to his voice, *Should've* replied, "Well, *Coach*, that's easier said than done."

Coach replied, "Look, anyone can say that you can move forward and forget about things, but, yes, you're right, that's easier said than done. And do you know why? Well let me tell you, because right now your mind is not only filled with negative thoughts from today, but from way back, as far back as when you were born, perhaps."

Should've felt himself welling up inside, it was as though the emotional floodgates were about to be opened. An instinctive feeling within *Coach* kicked in and he put a protective arm around *Should've*'s shoulder and said, "After a while these thoughts begin to weigh on you, they slow you down, and unless you get rid of them you'll never get to where you want to go. If you keep them, they will limit your ability to explore change."

The two sat quietly for a few minutes before *Coach* continued, "If you really want to start moving on, you have to get your mind to focus on new things; then you'll automatically let go of the negative events and situations that have been slowing you down on the track."

Should've's mood had shifted and he was now smiling, his temperament now a calmer disposition than it had been on the track and he even felt that what *Coach* was saying was beginning to make sense.

Coach went on, "Yes, explore, search for what's critical, and learn to make good decisions by trying to decipher the opportunity available to you. Remember there are often more options than you realise.

"Look for relevant evidence that could affect you and make the subtle shifts necessary, changes that take you towards your dream. When you start to do this, you begin to attract positive situations.

"Usually, people only get one good chance in a lifetime of effort. Even though, hundreds, thousands and even millions of chances are there for the taking in everyone's lifetime ... but usually there is only one once in a lifetime opportunity that comes along. So make the most of it. Stop defeating yourself, stop limiting yourself. Create the success you want and deserve in life.

"Consider this. There are three types of people in this world. Firstly, there are people who *make things happen*. Then there are people who *watch things happen*. Lastly, there are people who ask, *what happened*? Which do you want to be?"

Should've said, "Right now I know and understand that I have to focus on what I want to happen by searching and exploring for solutions. And now I know what this is, thanks to you, *Coach*."

Coach said, "Right! So, let's reshape your focus – starting from now."

Later that same day, *Coach* had an important message that he needed the whole group to understand, especially *Should've*.

He began his fifth rule:

RULE 5
Champions Have Clarity of Vision and a Clear Purpose

"Whilst you will be effective in the present, as a champion, you will take control of the future by planning for what may be over the horizon.

"You will make informed decisions about your chosen path based on relevant details that you see around you. While others become obsessed by things that are unimportant, you will have a great understanding of what is appropriate. You will possess the ability to assess a situation and plan for the future almost simultaneously.

"It is the skill of having a clear and decisive vision for the future whilst staying focused on the present that makes the real difference when it comes to performing under pressure."

This made huge sense to *Should've* because of the chat he had with *Coach*, it also struck a chord with the others.

"I kind of realised this, but it wasn't until I experienced it that I really understood the impact this would have on me. I have learned that I sometimes doubt myself, but when I have clarity, I can stay focused, and I believe more," said *Could've*.

This rule had also resonated with *Would've*, he really understood this message and the impact it would have on his desire. He was clear in his mind about what he really wanted. Now that he had chosen athletics over a football career, he felt more determined than ever. What confused him, though, was that, for some reason, he didn't really want to admit it.

Before they left, *Coach* handed each of the four his customary handwritten '*Coach* Quote'.

COACH QUOTE

Your focus determines your reality.

Rule 6

Champions Challenge the Process

This is my life

Things were progressing well and it was time for the National Championships. This race was a big deal in terms of the athletes learning to compete under pressure, particularly for *Should've* as this was a new environment and one in which *Coach* thought he might struggle. It was important for them to try to gain a place in the relay squad. They could do this by performing well in the individual race. *Coach* was fascinated to see how each of them would behave, for he knew that their mental attitude was now the only thing that would differentiate their results.

"In just a few hours from now, you will have the power to accomplish anything you set your mind to. You have total dominion over your race."

The pep talk from *Coach* was a powerful oration: "You are the only one in control of your destiny. You can, if you want, access your imagination."

This was more than just a pep talk, it was a lesson in one of the skills that *Coach* knew would be essential in all their preparations.

The day of the National Championships rather predictably mirrored the earlier smaller meeting, with just *Should've* underperforming.

Despite *Should've*'s poor race, the day had gone well. *Coach* realised that there was a possibility that two of the group (and maybe even three) might make the team for the sprint relay at the Olympic Games. This excited *Coach*, who saw a great opportunity to use this to build an even stronger dynamic within the already tight training group.

"What do you think about us competing in the Olympic relay, *Coach*?" asked *Did*.

"Yourself and *Could've* will be a huge asset to the relay team. Look at how much you have improved. This momentum can take you all the way. It is also a matter of focus. The relay in the Olympic Games takes place after the individual race. This could be a great secondary focus for you and may well add to your overall energy and determination at the Games.

"... this could be seen as a win–win situation," *Coach* said, in a very positive way."

"Sorry, say that again, *Coach*? said a confused *Did*.

"You can train with the other guys first, then apply your attention towards the individual race, before re-directing your focus to the relay," said *Coach*.

Grasping the gist of what *Coach* had meant, *Did* said, "Maybe."

"Many people I meet," *Coach* said, "set themselves up for a fall by creating impossible situations that bring about unlikely resolutions. This 'heads you win, tails I lose' attitude can only bring them failure and is the opposite to that of any champion I have worked with.

"Champions set themselves up for gain, regardless of a number of potential scenarios unfolding. You see, *Did*, all of you, as a group, are learning this and applying yourselves very well. I have been impressed by your development as a team and while there is still a long way to go, we've covered a lot of ground."

Did noticed how *Coach*'s language had changed since the early days of training. Although *Coach* had always believed in the group, he had now taken them up a level. The momentum of this move forward to them being potential Olympians had to be maintained, *Coach* needed to really peak and, ultimately, to maximise their performances. *Coach*'s job was to maintain this momentum and deal with any potential distractions along the way.

*****

One evening there was a different mood at the training track. Where the group would normally just do the session without question, on this particular evening there was unrest. For the first time, the athletes were not happy with *Coach*'s training suggestions. Due to what had been done before in this stage of their work, the athletes were expecting a race-distance, time-trial session which they would enjoy, as it would be a chance to see what was 'in the tank'. The problem began when *Coach* introduced the session for the evening which was something completely unexpected. He wanted very short races from varied starting positions – lying, sitting and other unusual positions — this was unorthodox at this time of the year – and *Coach* knew it.

Coach explained the big picture and the need for some right–brain thinking for this competitive session, as they were in a speed phase of their training – learning how to adapt and compete.

Coach knew that even though logical, sequential, rational and objective left–brain thinking was good, at times some random, intuitive and subjective right–brain thinking was useful because it was linked to achievement and success. When it comes to left and right–brain thinking, we all have a distinctive predilection for one of these styles of thinking. *Coach* knew that some, however, are more whole–brained and equally adept at both modes of thinking.

The negativity within the group showed when *Could've*,

surprisingly and abruptly, snapped with anger in his voice, "Just leave our training the way it used to be!" There was such venom in his voice that the other three pulled away and stood quietly, not moving.

Could've was taken aback at his outburst and proceeded to recriminate himself for acting so irrationally. He now felt his own self–judgment making him feel stupid, and immature.

Could've thought to himself, "This is not how a well–disciplined, potentially successful athlete is supposed to behave." He knew all eyes were on him, he just wanted the whole incident, and how he felt about it, to go away.

Could've didn't apologise, but in an effort to rejoin with the group he said, "Aw, come on. You were all whinging under your breath about it."

Coach said, "It is not my role to quell such dissent amongst you. However, it is my role to promote empowerment and to get you thinking for yourselves."

So now *Coach* had to pull them out of their negative mood and put his right–brain creativity to use to get them intrigued. *Coach* asked them all to stand at the starting line of the track. "Right," he said, with some authority in his voice, "Let me show you something - when I say 'go' I want you all to jump a distance of half a metre. GO!"

The four jumped, and because they were focusing on this task and the outcome, it took their minds off the negative mood they were in. Certainly what *Coach* had used here was a way to get them right–brained thinking.

"The truth is," *Coach* said, "most sprinters miss out on success by this distance, the distance between your head and your heart. Now, if you let your hot heads rule your hearts, then that is the distance you will lose by.

"When you decide to go ahead and do what needs to be done – despite your discomfort – you will experience the benefits," said *Coach*.

Coach knew that tensions were running high, after all, there was a lot at stake here. He knew that sometimes it was all too easy to give way to our feelings and abandon good judgment. Sometimes, when there is a rise in the path of destiny, it can block our view of what is on the other side. So, as we stand at the crossroads, all we can see is the immediate bliss – or soreness – that awaits.

What *Coach* was trying to do was take the athletes to a higher level of control. He wanted them to appreciate the importance of challenging common understanding. He wanted them to make their own rules, to take ownership of understanding from their own truths.

Somehow he needed to get them all to realise: all that was previously pleasurable can, in these stages, become painful; equally, that which was previously painful could now become pleasurable. *Coach* just had to show them the way. He did not want to lead them towards the pain of regret.

He said to them all, "When you decide to go ahead and challenge current understanding, despite the resistance it may bring, you will grow stronger because of it. It will help you to build your own evidence.

"It is action that creates motivation. I know I previously said to change outcomes you had to change your thought patterns. That still stands. But when you are in a situation where you have to step up to the plate, so to speak, then first you act, and then you experience the benefits.

"Well then, it is clear that the time to act is now. After all, if you don't make things happen for you, things will happen to you.

"You don't have to do a great deal at once." In an effort to put down this dissent from the group, *Coach* said something he knew would undermine their egos: "If it hurts, then baby steps will do. But, as you act, you will discover the incredible power that lies dormant within you."

After a short but heated chat about the different techniques *Coach* was using in this session, the athletes backed down and agreed to do the session.

Coach was noticing more changes in the behaviour of the group. He still noticed some weaknesses, but, very slowly, each athlete was beginning to see how they each behaved and how these subtly different aspects of their own personalities could present themselves as either strengths or weaknesses.

He knew that one of the fundamental steps in any change was this crucial awareness of behaviour. He knew that while there was ignorance or denial, things could never change.

What he really wanted was for the group to have the confidence and passion to search for change. This especially applied to *Should've*. However, they all needed to build a question into all their vocabulary. He wanted them all to ask the question "What if ...?"

He knew that simply asking themselves this question would prompt them all to explore.

Coach had a plan for everyone except *Did*. In fact, *Did* was part of the plan. *Coach* wanted to instil some extra confidence in them, in order for some of the athletes to overcome their fear of asking questions and challenging things in a positive way.

"What are the other three really afraid of?" *Coach* thought to himself. He knew that each athlete had a pet fear, but he really wanted to delve deep into each one's psyche to see what made them tick. And he intended to explore this in an unconventional way. In his mind he knew that fear was down to what might simply be lurking there, not necessarily what actually existed. In other words, this fear provides the block to performance not the actual problem. *Coach* knew that low levels of self-confidence stemmed from staying in your comfort zone and fearing failure – hence the avoidance of taking risks.

Sometimes it was the fear of what could go wrong, and sometimes it was the fear of tackling something new that was holding some of the athletes back.

It was clear to *Coach* that *Did* was succeeding because he could eliminate anxiety and panic by asking questions.

By not asking questions some of the athletes didn't have enough information to be confident in themselves, and as a consequence their tendency was to focus on what could go wrong

This lack of focus was what *Coach* was planning to concentrate on. He wanted to change their thoughts, to get them to start thinking about how things could work out.

Coach could see that some of the athletes, at times, would go into a negative tailspin, being out of control of the direction they intended.

Coach was hoping his plan would work on the subconscious minds of *Could've*, *Should've* and *Would've*. Hopefully, they would pick up on these new thoughts. They could then begin enjoying life, develop greater confidence and enjoy the success and happiness they deserved.

It was the last day of training for the week: time to put his plan into action. He figured that this would give them a chance to explore the concept on their rest day.

He decided to chat about this with *Did*. "There is something that you do very well, and I would like the rest of the group to do it too."

"Yeah, what's that, *Coach*?"

"You naturally ask 'what if?', and you also have a tendency to ask 'why?' a lot. You seem to do this equally, whether you are thriving or you are struggling. This is what I want the other guys to do too.

"I see *Could've* not doing this through his lack of belief, *Should've* through his resistance to change and *Would've* because he's stuck in his comfort zone and he doesn't have your passion for improvement."

"What can I do to help, *Coach*?"

"I'm not sure, but between us we can help them to see the impact this can have," *Coach* said as he thought about a possible solution.

As *Coach* often would, he made notes in his diary; this time, he made them specifically about this trait, about how he observed it in *Did* and how he was instigating a plan to get it across to the whole group.

Coach went to the changing room where the others would be after their session, left his diary in full view on the top of his bag and went back outside.

After the session, he asked *Did* to walk around the track with him while the others went back to the changing room.

As they walked, *Coach* revealed what he had done, "I have left my notes open on the exact page where I have written about this trait of asking 'what if?' and 'why?' and what we discussed. Right now, the others will be reading my notes."

Did asked, "Don't you trust them?"

Coach replied, "Of course I trust them, but they do so out of curiosity more than anything else. It's like a schoolboy trying to find out the exam results before they are posted. Just curiosity, nothing more."

"What do you think they'll do when they read them?" asked a curious *Did*.

"They will read these notes, probably instigated by *Could've*, and then they are likely to challenge me. Please, say nothing about this," *Coach* replied.

After walking the lap, *Coach* walked straight to the changing room, picked up his diary and closed it. "Have a great weekend, all," *Coach* said as he picked up his bag and opened the door. He was just about to leave when, as he predicted, *Could've* shouted, "Wait, *Coach*!"

"What's up?" *Coach* asked innocently.

"I read it!" fumed *Could've*.

"Read what?" *Coach* asked, as if he didn't already know.

"Your diary."

"You shouldn't have. They are my notes, for me alone. They won't mean anything to you, not out of context," said *Coach*.

"Why did you write that?"

Coach saw the irony in this question, as he had planted the notes there in order to get *Could've* to ask this sort of question; surely *Coach*'s plan wasn't that easy? "It was just an observation, *Could've*. You have much talent and my responsibility is to optimise it. Now that you have read it, I suppose I should explain more. For now, though, please think about it over the weekend and we can chat more on Monday."

The four athletes left the session once more, with something to think about, *Could've* perhaps more so than the others.

On the Monday, *Coach* asked the group to join him in the clubhouse, as he had something important to say:

RULE 6
Champions Challenge the Process

"You will do this by constantly exploring your territory – by asking, 'What are my options?' You are very creative and will often ask, 'Is that really the best way of doing this?' and then you will see a new angle, maybe a better way. You will never take 'no' for an answer. Instead, you will feel compelled to come up with solutions.

"No doubt, you will often wake up early, thinking 'Let's go, I've got it!' Champions are always looking for a better way. It is this type of creativity, desire, passion and belief that will ensure renewable and sustained success."

Coach's plan had worked! *Could've* would be the catalyst to bringing this positive change about. *Did* was delighted that the others had begun to accept this trait, but then he assessed himself in a new way too. In the back of *Did*'s mind there were niggling thoughts that maybe they had not done enough work on their start. "Surely this is what *Coach* is talking about?" he thought to himself.

He had never really felt comfortable in the start position, but had not said anything. This left *Did* feeling less confident than he could about this part of his race. He also felt less in control than he probably could, or should.

Did was looking for a better way, but was worried that

Coach would not like to hear his doubts. Now he understood that, to have a truly successful mentality, you must never hide something that you feel is right. That if you feel strongly about something, you should always speak up.

The great thing was that it wasn't too late and that this subtle change was a great way of tweaking what was becoming a really solid basis for a good performance.

Did thought back to the latest 'Coach Quote' he had been given and, suddenly, it all made sense.

COACH QUOTE

See it, feel it, trust it!

Rule 7

Champions Take Action

If not now, when?

Something had been bothering *Coach* about *Should've* ever since they'd started training together.

Coach was happy that he understood the importance of taking responsibility, but saw that there was still something missing. He saw that *Should've* would talk very intuitively about observations that he had made, yet continued acting without change. In other words, he was aware, but then ignored his own thoughts.

Coach was pleased that he was beginning to observe, at least, and that he now at least noticed the small changes he could make. Maybe that talk he'd had with *Should've* about focus was starting to pay dividends.

It became clear, at least to *Coach*, what the next step should be. The group were at the gym and were in the middle of a fairly gruelling workout.

"You're looking good today, *Should've*," *Coach* praised.

"Thanks, *Coach*. I'm pleased; that was a new PB squat."

"I like the way you decided to go for it. It wasn't planned, but you felt good and you went for it. I like that."

Should've felt good about being congratulated by *Coach*, as he knew he'd only do this if he genuinely meant it.

"What next?" *Coach* asked.

"Add those weights on to what's already on the bar, I fancy another PB," said *Should've*.

Coach had discreetly left a couple of the smaller weights

in the gym next to the lifting area in the hope that *Should've* would decide to go for it, and he had taken the bait.

"Great, let's do it." *Coach* said enthusiastically.

"My bar," *Should've* commanded as he took control of this now larger total weight.

Coach knew he had planned this the right way and saw it was important to encourage *Should've* through this in order to positively reinforce this new and effective behaviour.

Should've successfully completed his set of exercises with the heavier weight and as he replaced the bar back on the supporting rack he said, "I'll leave it there."

"Great job!" *Coach* reinforced the praise with a pat on *Should've*'s shoulder.

The truth was, this was well within *Should've*'s capability and *Coach* knew this. However, he didn't let on that he had planned the whole thing because he saw the huge benefit in reinforcing a small gain when *Should've* had taken the initiative and executed a task effectively.

Coach believed that, by taking small steps and looking for easy wins, *Should've* might just begin, at his own pace, to take control and initiate change.

Coach wanted to show *Should've* how to stay in the 'success zone', so he asked if he could spare him a few minutes. When they got to *Coach*'s office he pulled open his desk drawer and took out what looked like a battered steel tray.

"Ever play marbles?" asked *Coach*.

Should've laughed nervously: surely *Coach* hadn't brought him to the office to play marbles? "Yeah, as a kid I did," he cautiously replied.

"Good," said *Coach* as he cleared a pile of paperwork from the desk and placed the tray there. "Have you ever heard of the reticular activating system?"

Should've tried to contain himself as he could see how

serious *Coach* was, but he still let out a snort of laughter!

"Yes, yes, I know it's a convoluted name, but let me show you something. Here." *Coach* passed *Should've* a handful of marbles, his face completely straight. "Roll one to me across the tray."

Should've obliged, but as much as he tried rolling the marble across the tray it would find its own level in one of the indents and settle there. By the time *Should've* had used up all of the marbles, each of the tray's indentations had a marble in it; not one marble had reached *Coach*'s side of the tray.

"What has happened on the tray symbolises how the same mechanism is used in our brain when seeking out something, even at a subconscious level, you could call it a kind of a selective attention that we're not aware of," said *Coach*.

"Yeah, it reminds me of when I was a kid, all that moving around and falling into grubby little hollows in life," said *Should've* as he let some of his past come out.

"Have you ever noticed," asked *Coach*, "that if you drive a particular model of car, you often notice the same model car on the road when you are out driving; in fact, it can seem as though there are a great number of the same model car, even though, in reality, there may not be?"

Should've said, "Spot on, *Coach*! But what's that got to do with what we are doing here?"

"Transfer this same mechanism to success," said *Coach*, "and you will find that when you are in the success zone, you are creating and attracting success – you cannot help but come out of everything smelling of roses. That is the frame of mind, just like the marbles finding the hollows. Feel the success and you become successful. Feed positive thoughts and beliefs into your subconscious and you will turbo–charge yourself for success."

Should've said, "Turbo–charge? Now that's something I could do with. But how will I recognise when I am bordering on the success zone?"

"By creating a success-oriented mindset then you cannot help but stay in the success zone. You will recognise any set of circumstances that will lead to success and, time after time, you will follow the template of success in an effortless way," said *Coach*.

"So say I want to attract a positive event into my life, how could I do it?" asked *Should've*.

"When you take a moment to appreciate the positive things and to fill your mind with positive thoughts, you begin to attract positive events, people and situations into your life. Try it out. You'll see," said *Coach*.

*****

Back at the track things continued to progress well. One afternoon, *Coach* pointed someone out to the four athletes. This man was doing some warm–ups at the far end of the stadium. *Coach* said to the group, "See that man? He's here from overseas. He's one of the top men from a specialist unit, and he too trains like an Olympian. His name is March."

The athletes looked astounded: if this man drew *Coach*'s admiration, then he had to be something special to merit such an accolade.

In the past, *Coach* had met many athletes who became stimulated by simple fun and often competitive training sessions. That is why *Coach* was going to make this training session fun, stimulating and exciting, with plenty of right–brain thinking.

Coach addressed the group: "I have to admit, I may have bitten off more than I can chew over something."

What he said next was music to their ears, "I was dining with that gentleman yesterday evening, and we got talking about levels of training and fitness. I mentioned how fit you all are and how you could beat any man in his unit.

"I have to admit, I got rather drawn in. I was challenged to a wager."

"What was it?" asked *Did*.

"I'm not sure I want to tell you."

"Aw, come on, *Coach*!" *Should've* implored.

"Okay. I have bet my car." *Coach* loved his car.

"You've done what? That's crazy, why would you do that?" *Could've* chuckled as he asked this but inside felt great fear of the pressure it created.

"If the four of you lose, then March will drive home in my car. And keep it"

"And if he loses?" asked *Would've*.

"Ah, that's a good one. He has to travel up to the next meeting you're competing at ..."

"Is that it?" *Did* asked.

"... and he has to wear the mascot's suit for the afternoon, while cheering you all on."

"Yeah!" they all shouted.

The bet seemed out of balance as this could be a huge physical loss for *Coach* and only a humiliation for March. Strangely, they all felt more motivated by the thought of both.

Coach waved the man over and introduced them.

"Guys, this is March," said *Coach*.

Coach explained that it was agreed that the fitness competition was going to be similar to the test they used to select candidates for the unit March trained. Very gruelling!

The four athletes were focused on only two things: saving *Coach*'s car and seeing March wear the mascot's outfit.

Although March was now alone with four complete

strangers, in a strange way he felt that they were connected in this shared goal.

Somehow, word had got around about this bizarre fitness competition ... and about the forfeits! Even the groundsman came out to watch.

At the age of fifty–four, March had the strength of a mountain lion. None of the athletes knew his age, except for *Coach*, of course.

In the first fitness test – a balancing one leg squat, March was showing off in selling his moves with ease, and not even struggling.

"Looks like we've underestimated him," *Should've* thought to himself.

Could've looked sloppy in the first test. It really took the joy away from the exercise that the others were going to have to do!

Everyone knew that when you are looking for a test of co–ordination, speed, balance and strength to add to a fitness routine, advantage can be gained by finding one that's harder for other people than it is for you. March had certainly done this and claimed victory in this first test which was about slow strength and agility; not the athletes' forte.

The small crowd of spectators had swelled quickly from a few dozen to well over a hundred, and the closeness of the crowd put a rather different spin on this event. This 'training session' had now become a competition with a growing crowd of cheering spectators! After two or three fluffed tests, the four athletes really started to focus because they were getting beaten.

March was leading the group, he'd performed these tests frequently and it showed. One test was called the Stalder press, one of the most extraordinary moves in fitness, and one that very few athletes can do. It is performed by placing your hands between your legs and pressing up so that only your hands are touching the floor. Then, you have to work your way from that position to a handstand position! Of course, March won this one, as he said, 'hands down' and the crowd's applause was not music to the ears of the four athletes.

Should've felt that the mainly partisan crowd should have been cheering the 'home' team, not March. This was the exact instinct *Coach* wanted to arouse in *Should've*, the competitive instinct. *Coach* was attentive to the body language of his group, and he learned a lot from what he saw.

Coach knew that this would work like a charm: the plan he had instigated with March – using distractions to sabotage the focus levels of the athletes – was now paying dividends. What the four athletes didn't know was that *Coach* had actually asked his long-time coaching friend March for a favour ... not a wager!

So as to rub salt in the athletes' wounds, March said to the crowd, with a laugh, "I'm probably going to have to wait until the next show to demonstrate my other skills."

It was *Could've*'s turn to perform in the next test, one where they had to hold a heavy shot–putt out at arm's length, and hold it, against the clock. He performed well. Next came *Would've*'s turn and, during it, March said out loud to *Could've*, "Is that your sister?" Pointing to *Would've* who was deep in concentration.

Would've was on fire with pain, but on hearing this he gave more than he thought possible, beating even March's performance.

During the next few tests, March was fully focused, as the lead between him was being reduced. Then it came to the maximum strength test. Simply, the participant starts at a relatively heavy weight and, if successful in completing the simple dead-lift, attempts an even heavier weight.

Should've was on his second phase of this test, using a weight close to his maximum. His face was contorted as he fought through the pain. March said to him, "People always say, 'You're going to look like your mom when you're older.' I think you look like her now."

Should've threw the weight to the floor, and *Coach* had to quickly intervene and usher *Should've* away from March.

When it came to *Could've*'s turn, March said, "You better hurry up here. You are not getting any younger!"

Could've didn't flicker. *Coach* liked what he saw: each athlete under pressure. He knew he still had work to do with *Should've*'s ability to accept change, but at least when he had ushered *Should've* away he raised a laugh when he whispered in his ear, "Just wait until the dancing round!"

In the speed and acceleration test, March said to *Did*, "No pressure on you here then. You'd better be feeling good!"

Did was so deeply focused on the task that he didn't even hear March. *Coach* noticed this and was impressed at *Did*'s level of focus. This 'training' session was certainly about the power of focus. It was *Coach*'s goal to cultivate the group's ability to focus on the task at hand and block out all distractions – press, TV, crowd noise and even personal insults, as this is what they would often face during some of the more important competitions.

Coach typically encouraged athletes to work with sport psychologists to learn how to focus intently through a form of self–hypnosis, but also fully understood his own impact on this vital skill by assisting in nurturing all the important psychological characteristic needed to become a champion. Today had been a prime example of this.

At the end of the tests the scores were totted up – the dynamic this had created was incredibly powerful for all to see.

Coach thought to himself, "Yes, it was worthwhile holding this training session ... it's only a car!"

"*Coach, Coach*! We won by three points" gushed an excited *Should've*.

March had genuinely given his best, and when *Coach* told his group that they had done well to beat a 54-year-old, they were astonished at March's fitness levels.

Coach then explained to the group what he had done. How he had created this dynamic with the input of an old friend.

"This stimulus has had a marked effect on your focus, your determination and you have all applied yourselves more effectively. What I would like you to do is to nurture this feeling. I want you to understand that this feeling is purely as a result of how you perceived a situation. This is something you can, now that you know this, access at will – *any time you want*."

Before leaving, March told the group a story, which he said would serve them well in understanding why they must always focus on who they are.

"One day a man was walking through the jungle when he chanced upon a lion cub. He took it back to his farm and put it with a cow that had just given birth. The young lion cub suckled from the cow and was soon accepted into the herd.

"As the lion cub grew larger and stronger, he developed the mindset of a cow. He would chew at the grass, eat oats and when it rained he would moo and lay down with the rest of the herd, just as the rest of the cows did. When the day drew to a close, the farmer would march him, along with the rest of the herd, back to the cowshed so as to be ready for the early morning's milking.

"When the cows were milked in the morning, the lion would also stand in line, just like the rest of them. The farmer would say to the lion, 'Not your turn yet.'

"The lion spent his life as a cow, he knew nothing else. As the lion grew older the farmer thought about putting him into an animal sanctuary so that he could see out his remaining time with other lions.

"Eventually, the time came for the lion to be let loose with the other lions, and as he looked out from the holding cage he could see some magnificent creatures. They were so regal, and walked around like they owned the place, roaring and yawning in order to show their big carnivore's teeth. They had such big manes, which made them look like they were wearing king's robes.

"The farmer had sent a cow along as company in case the lion became nervous. The lion asked his cow friend, what were these regal creatures he was seeing? The cow looked at the lion quizzically: 'Don't you know? These are lions. Kings of the jungle. They are from the Great Plains of Africa, they are one of the most formidable animals on the planet, and they belong in the jungle. We are cows; we belong in the fields of a farm.'

"It was obvious that the lion wasn't going to settle in, and the other lions shunned him. Soon he was returned to the farm, and he was pleased to be back where he felt that he belonged. The lion lived out the rest of his life as a cow, as that was his mindset.

"The lion never really had the opportunity to discover his real birthright – King of the jungle – and this is often the problem with those who have potential. They never recognise who they really are and never get to express their full potential.

"Today, you have all shown me that you have the hearts of lions."

March and the athletes parted on friendly terms, and even *Should've* gave March a friendly hug.

Before *Could've* left for the day, *Coach* said to him,

"You took March's taunts well; now you may understand why I added that extra weight to your backpacks when we went on that mountain trek all those months ago. You were pushed into an uncomfortable zone by me on the mountain, and you were also in that same zone when March applied the pressure today. You remember when I talked to you about the *adaptation zone* on the mountain? Well this is the same thing and you handled it well; well done."

The following day, during their warm–up, *Coach* reminded the group that he was pleased with how everything was going.

"Get yourselves ready, we'll start in forty minutes or so. I just need to make a few phone calls."

Coach knew there was a storm brewing and that soon it would be raining. He didn't really need to make phone calls, he just wanted to observe the group's behaviour for future reference and see how they might make the necessary adjustments.

What happened next was music to *Coach*'s ears.

"*Coach*, could we switch the sessions around and do the gym session today and the track tomorrow? We could then go to the gym now. We'll get soaked otherwise. It's a quality track session that's needed and I'd be happy to change the plans to make this as effective as possible. The forecast is better for tomorrow, I just checked," *Should've* requested.

"Yes! I mean, yep, sure, no probs." *Coach* was delighted that *Should've* had observed this, had initiated change and then, most importantly, acted upon it.

Coach realised that his role was changing, evolving from that of a teacher to a more collaborative role. This pleased him immensely as he knew that his ultimate goal was to make himself redundant. He wanted them to take ownership of their destiny. This process had begun.

It pleased *Coach* that *Should've* would now explore

change and act upon it naturally and maybe he could role–model this kind of behaviour to the rest of the group.

Coach understood that it wasn't enough to recognise successful traits; it was acting upon them that was most important.

The very next day, *Coach* took the opportunity to talk to the group before their training. He explained that:

RULE 7
Champions Take Action

"It is one thing to know what should be done, it is another to do it.

"It pleases me that you are all able to make decisions and to take action immediately. You are beginning to make things happen. I like how you will be pro–active, have a plan or a vision, and will react and change immediately to circumstances along the way. It is true, therefore, to say that champions never ignore the obvious, always act promptly, and strive to inspire action in others."

Would've had noticed that *Coach*'s tone had changed and that he was beginning to believe in the group. This was coming through even in the language he had chosen when introducing 'The Rules'. He also noticed the changes in *Did* too, and wondered where he got his motivation from.

While *Would've* was thinking, "Ought I or oughtn't I?" *Did* had gone ahead and done it.

Would've took the chance to chat to *Should've*, who he saw as being similar to himself. "What do you make of all this? I can see what *Coach* is saying. Is it something that we are born to do, or can we learn it? This is what makes me wonder if I should commit to developing this trait."

"*Coach* would say that *whether you choose to believe you will succeed or you choose to believe you will fail, you will probably be right*. I always seem to find myself looking for reasons to 'not do' something, but I'm beginning to see that this is a decision that I make. Now, when I catch myself doing it, I stop and take a moment to look at other options," said *Should've*.

The two could see this from both perspectives, which was a huge shift for both of them: they had grown in awareness. Now it was time to do something about it.

Both athletes left feeling determined to make this small, but powerful change – to take action

Coach had left them all with another handwritten '*Coach* Quote' to add to the others.

COACH QUOTE

A barrier is only a limitation when you perceive it as one.

Rule 8

Champions are always Keen to Learn, Keen to Enquire and Keen to Listen and Understand

Two ears ... one mouth

It was exactly twelve months until the start of the Olympic Games and, once again, the team was at a training camp. It was time for *Coach* to 'up the ante' and so he had organised a special overseas training trip. This was not only a chance for the group to train in great weather, but to train while surrounded by some other top athletes too.

There was one athlete in particular that *Coach* wanted to introduce to the group: his name was Swift, and he was the most successful athlete on the planet. Swift was the reigning Olympic and world champion and, at *Coach*'s request, he had come to watch the team train.

The athletes had travelled together and this was the first day of training – a light session to recover from the journey. After the session they all went out to eat. *Coach* saw this as an opportunity for the athletes to learn from the best; he hoped that they'd see Swift as a role model and really try to understand him.

Just before meeting Swift, *Coach* singled out *Did* and pulled him to one side and told him, "Now you have the chance to learn from him ... and to become a champion yourself!"

Coach had a specific reason for doing this, it was because he felt that out of the four athletes, *Did* had what it took to go all the way to the top – to become a champion. He knew he couldn't guarantee a win, so when *Coach* referred to *Did* becoming a champion, he referred to the way he would act, respond to situations, aspire, think, feel and impact others. This is what *Coach* knew was the mark of a true champion; this was success. The other three were certainly champions in the making, but right now it was *Did* who was showing the most promise. The other three might, *Coach* hoped, eventually reach this stage too.

Over dinner, Swift shared some fascinating stories with the group, which pleased *Coach* as he knew the power of learning from others that had 'been there, done that'.

"I really like the dynamic of your team, *Coach*, and I can see that making a huge difference to both the team and the individuals within it. I have known *Coach* for many years and have always enjoyed talking to him and picking his brains. You have a perfect set up," Swift said.

The first thing that *Could've* noticed was that Swift seemed like a pretty down–to–earth sort of guy. He hadn't expected this.

"How did you start out in your career?" *Did* asked Swift.

"I watched the Games as a kid, and it seemed like my destiny. I didn't know if I'd be good enough, but, growing up, it was the one thing that I would dream about. I used to catch myself dreaming about being at the Games and thriving in the ultimate high–pressure environment. Then I met *my* great *Coach*, the hard work began and everything started to fall into place."

"*Did* you ever doubt yourself?" asked *Could've*.

"Of course I did, we all do from time to time but I saw this as part of my development," Swift replied and then asked, "Do you?"

Could've didn't answer, he just smiled.

"What was the factor that made the biggest difference?" *Should've* asked.

"I think that would be learning to reinvent myself, year in, year out, in order to retain the freshness to be inspired. I sometimes used to find myself in a rut and found it hard to climb out of it. Looking back, the one thing that was very important was the ability to explore change. Now, I see the ability to *assess, adapt and evolve* as the most important factor in any athlete's development."

"Were you always inspired to train hard and dream of success?" *Would've* asked.

"No, not always, but I saw this as being similar to belief, in that it might need some work. It was easy to feel passionate and confident during the good times. It was during the tough times that I was ultimately challenged. And, like you, I love a challenge."

The group smiled, lost in their thoughts due to the fact that Swift's words really resonated with them personally.

Coach listened in but took a back seat as the group seemed to be doing exactly what he had hoped – listening.

"Speaking from your experience, what would you say we should aim to do?" *Did* probed.

"Never stop learning, never stop asking questions, always think outside the box. Have you ever tried to see if the light was on in the fridge when the door's closed?"

The four laughed at the absurdity of this question, but saw the relevance. Swift continued, "Of course you have and so have I. You do this because you are fascinated, not just as to *what* and *why*, but *how*."

Should've was the only one who wondered to himself why he had never done this.

Coach was mulling something over, so he threw a question to Swift which he wanted the group to think about. "How do you handle negative stress?"

"I know you know the answer to that. You helped me learn this." Swift was perceptive, and went on, "I guess this is a question for everyone but you, *Coach*. Well, imagine how successful you would be if you were full of energy all day long, regardless of whether it's early in the morning or last thing at night. Day in and day out.

"I mean, can you imagine coming into training the day after competing on the track, and still feeling full of energy? Then going home and finishing off putting up those shelves. You just don't have time for stress.

"If you don't know how to control them properly, single thoughts can make you stressed. Stress will only arise out of how you perceive a situation and, after all, how you perceive is your choice. *Coach* taught me this many years ago and it's true.

"You see, to a large extent, the amount of success you have in your life is determined by your energy levels. I just don't have time for negative stress. I am always raising my energy levels. I always feel good, because how I feel is my choice.

"I guess if you are underprepared and you go to do something that takes willpower and drive, you might get anxious. Your heart might start pounding, and that might be your subconscious mind remembering when you tried the same thing on a previous occasion and maybe failed at it. If you get into the fail zone then you have to kick yourself back out of it with positive thoughts. Otherwise you can fail due to the fear of failure. Your mind is telling you, 'Don't do that again. Don't get rejected. Stop now.'

"These are stored emotions, and what happens is that when a situation resembles something that you previously failed at, stress kicks in and emotions associated with losing are released within you. By raising your energy levels you just don't give these negative stored emotions a chance to speak to you.

"I'm not saying that I never feel nervous, I do! The point is that it is positive nerves, a type of powerful energy that will surge through your veins and make you focus. The key is to channel any nervous response in a positive way."

Swift was entertaining and informative throughout the evening, and he seemed genuinely interested in the four athletes.

At first, *Could've* listened, but he wanted to share his own experiences. In an attempt to impress Swift he said, "Has *Coach* told you I ran a PB in training last week? I'm in really good shape and looking forward to the next competition."

Coach acknowledged *Could've* and smiled at Swift. Both *Coach* and Swift knew the reason for this. *Coach* was disappointed that *Could've* still felt the need to talk about his own success. He knew what *Could've* was doing, that he desperately wanted Swift to respect him. This showed a real lack of awareness in *Could've* and it was clear that this lack of self–restraint needed further attention. For now, though, it was appropriate to let it pass as there were many positives to take from the evening. It would be inappropriate to focus on this just now.

Did showed he was developing – he asked Swift, "What is the most important rule for success, based upon your experience and expertise, that will most transform people's lives?"

Although a similar question had already been asked, *Coach* had been in deep thought on other matters, but now he picked up on the key words and was impressed with the relevance of this question. He waited to see if Swift would answer in the way he expected.

In his head, Swift had run through all of the past expertise he had encountered, and even a few of his successes and how he had arrived at them, and answered, "In short, surround yourself with positive–minded people. Make acquaintance with those who will encourage you on the path to your goals, and find ways to spend more time with them. Share your aspirations only with those who will support you, not those who will respond with doubt or lack of interest."

Coach put it another way, "I agree; try always to mix with positive–minded people as a means to tap into your unexploited potential."

As the evening progressed, Swift recalled a story relating to an Olympian that had also been taught by *Coach*.

"I knew one athlete who felt he didn't have the personal willpower to be a success on his own: he needed a goal. So, before a race he would say to some of the athletes he knew well, 'If you beat me, I'll come and clean your house for a day'."

Coach thought he would throw in one of his own stories. *Coach* recalled a story to the group of an ancient Olympian who was so sure of his victory in a running event that he had his victory statue made before the Games were even held. When he won, he was able to dedicate his statue on the same day

This story from *Coach* seemed to go straight over *Did*'s head as he asked Swift about the athlete he had talked of: "Was he ever beaten?"

"You bet he wasn't, at least not when he gave out this challenge, anyway!"

Coach chipped in, "This is called *willpower leveraging*. You use a little bit of willpower to establish a consequence that will literally compel you to keep your commitment."

"Really!" said an excited *Did*. "I just wish I had his way of thinking ...." he trailed off.

Swift loved a challenge, he liked the energy of the group and he was drawn in by *Did*'s open thought.

"I'll tell you what, why don't we do something similar? How about this.... If you beat me I will donate a large amount of money to a charity of your choice."

Swift liked *Coach*'s *willpower leveraging theory* and thought he would apply it to his own situation.

Perhaps this was something Swift would one day regret: just as much as he was applying the *willpower leveraging theory* to himself, he was also creating a powerful incentive for *Did*.

Swift added, "A successful athlete has to be able to build flexibility into their expectations, to adjust things as they improve." This was all about being able to adapt.

One of the things that struck *Coach* about Swift was how, even now, he was periodically re-evaluating his goals and plans, even during his leisure time, such as this evening.

Coach made a mental note about 'evaluating your plan', "It's about being able to identify any part that isn't working well, this may simply mean allocating more time to complete a specific task or part of a task."

He then made another... "It is important to the group that they acknowledge even partial successes. Running a PB at a shorter distance during training is cause for celebration, even if the original goal of running a PB over a longer distance failed."

The discussions had certainly stimulated lots of appropriate thinking, even in *Coach*.

The evening continued and the discussions developed until *Coach* realised the time. "Probably best to get the bill now, guys. It's getting late. No doubt Swift will join us again some other time?" Then, to himself, he added, "Probably at the next Olympic Games – so be prepared!"

"For sure, that'd be great. Thanks for a wonderful evening," said Swift.

Overall, the evening had been a huge success. However,

Coach had observed that while *Would've* seemed to be comfortable in Swift's company, he preferred to talk about social stuff more than sport. He had seen before that some athletes set themselves up for failure by either having unrealistic goals or, as in *Would've*'s case, not really following through the ones he set. *Coach* knew that with *Would've*, he had to see and believe in what he was able to do to keep motivated. There was still work to be done for *Would've* to have this clarity and ensuing passion, but progress had been made.

Did had listened, asked questions and tried to get a feel for what Swift really meant.

Swift had gone and it was time for *Coach* to add the eighth Rule:

RULE 8

Champions are always Keen to Learn, Keen to Enquire and Keen to Listen and Understand

"Clever people, like you, value relationships and develop a team of people around you whom you trust. You will understand the power of perspective and, therefore, will be keen to understand the ideas of others.

"Champions do this by seeking to consult and understand others and by networking well. You will not only learn from the relevant people around you, but will be able to reapply their skills in an even better way.

> *"The point here is not the ability to store or regurgitate facts that you have learned from others, it is the application of the understanding of the key principles that matters. Sustained performance is not about learning something parrot fashion, it is about understanding others, interpreting and then applying knowledge.*
>
> *"Champions also consult opinion across industries. It is never about who is right or wrong, it is about what is best."*

After this evening's meeting, *Did* now knew exactly what could be learned from others and what impact it could have on his performance.

Could've became aware that this wasn't naturally something that he did well. He was only interested in drawing energy from putting other people down, but was beginning to realise that he did this due to his lack of confidence.

Initially this had made *Could've* feel sad, as he realised that he had been behaving inappropriately. He looked back at some of *Coach*'s other rules and realised that he simply had to take action and to explore a better way.

He wasn't quite sure what this might look like, but he was keen to learn and to make amends.

*****

Swift had gone home and as they were about to say their goodbyes for the evening, *Coach* wanted to leave the group with a powerful and difficult message on the subject of 'enhanced' performance: "There are athletes who have won, but won by cheating, through various means, drugs, for example. They call themselves champions, but they are not. They are parasites, feasting on the soul of the sport."

Coach looked to the sky and continued: "There is a wasp that lives in the jungles of South America that injects a 'love' venom into its host, a caterpillar. The host then craves the wasp and seeks it's companionship through to its demise. This is what some of the cheats in our sport do. They come back to the sport after a drug ban and compel the sport to forgive them, claiming that they are reformed. Drug cheats to me should be banned for life. They have brought more damage to our sport than they will ever know. I wanted you all to know, this is where I stand on this."

"The only enhancement you will need is an honest and effective *consultative council*," *Coach* said passionately.

As they left, he then handed out his handwritten '*Coach* Quote'.

COACH QUOTE

Act like a Champion in all aspects of your life.

Rule 9

Champions Never Give Up

Unexpended effort

could've   should've   would've   did

Coach really understood the group well now and had started working at overcoming their limiting behaviours. He had known of their individual traits since day one and each athlete had made significant gains since then....

Could've had lacked belief

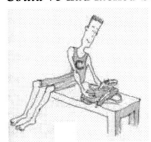

Coach had used phrases with *Could've* such as: "You looked very comfortable today, why's that?", "It must have felt great leading the group in that session", "People really look up to you when you do well".

145

Coach was beginning to make some inroads into how *Could've* was taking ownership with the positive dialogue he was applying in a subliminal way. Now was the time for *Could've* to start manifesting the champion within, and thereafter *Coach* didn't see any need to use bolstering phrases to boost *Could've*'s confidence.

Could've's lack of belief in himself was consigned to the past. A new dawning was beginning to emerge for him.

Should've generally hated change

Coach was pleased with the way he had gone about instilling acceptance of change in *Should've*. *Coach* had slowly brought *Should've* from an environment with no changes to one where changes were gradual and *Should've* was accepting of this.

When *Coach* changed the start time by five or ten minutes, or changed the venue and training sessions at the last minute, *Should've*, without realising it, was starting to get used to adapting and felt more comfortable. With each change, *Coach* would apply positive reinforcement.

It was now dawning on *Should've* that an awareness of his resistance to these small adaptations would also bring a deeper understanding of the consequences of not taking action.

Coach knew that this was a critical phase and that any resistance to subtle shifts would soon fall away as *Should've* was now facing up to dealing with things that were bothering him and learning to look at things differently – to find solutions by being flexible.

Would've had lacked passion

In the case of *Would've*'s lack of passion, *Coach* took the time to ask lots of questions, all of which contained one word – *why*? If *Coach* could find out *why*, he'd find the key to unlocking a passion in *Would've* that would be unstoppable.

Coach studied him at every session and probably talked to him more than to any of the other athletes. *Coach* knew that he'd need to understand *Would've* in order to influence his core values so as to turn them around.

Once *Coach* gained an understanding of *Would've*, he reinforced everything he heard. Every time he gave *Coach* an insight as to why he was there, *Coach* would embellish it and say it back to him. He was clever enough to do this in a way that wasn't obvious to *Would've*.

Slowly, *Would've* began to feel more passionate, more committed and more hungry for that higher level of performance that *Coach* had alluded to.

Did was single–minded

Coach spotted a win–win scenario in helping *Did* to see the importance of working in a team. If he got the dynamic right, he could create a situation where all of the team members could benefit from each other. This was the ultimate goal for *Coach*. He called it *'the magic*

of alignment'. This was when the whole was greater than the sum of the parts.

Coach would look for teamwork opportunities and make *Did* an integral part of this. *Did*, as he himself knew, wasn't as talented as some of the others but he had a great attitude. His greatest chance of Olympic glory was if he bought into the team and strived even harder as a result of it. In order to make this happen, *Coach* needed to continue to teach *Did* the power of interdependence.

Coach understood that *Did* would need to be able to trust himself to read situations and apply himself effectively.

"Independent people like you have the ability to take responsibility. Once you learn to operate within a team, you will need to appreciate the importance of roles and how they relate to your responsibilities.

"The challenge comes when circumstances change and you need to adapt as a unit. When you truly become interdependent, it will be like you have developed another sense, a sense that means you will know what to do and when to do it, and that will help the team to thrive.

"The biggest difference between individual and team success is that when you operate truly effectively as a team, you will begin to only make decisions on one basis – the team. For a group to operate in this way requires a shift in awareness away from any individual gain."

While *Did* was beginning to understand the impact of awareness for himself, it was not clear to him how this would work in a group. He trusted himself, he knew why he made decisions and would do this intuitively and effectively all the time.

Coach said to *Did*, "You know, you'd be stunned if you

knew just how many people are ready and willing to help you, if only you'd define your need and ask for help.

"Within a team framework, there is a single mindset: one belief and one goal. There should be no need to beg people to help. You simply ask your team for help, like the friend who has done everything in his power to achieve success and now needs that final push from a buddy.

"If you want to access the mind power of those who can help you to reach your goals, you have to be aware of what makes others tick. You have to be thankful for the inner workings of their brain. Once you can walk their mental map, you can help direct them too.

"In order to develop a winning mindset you need to make mindful decisions in everyday interactions. Every word and body movement must be natural, but deliberate. Your reactions to this information have to be focused and attentive."

*****

It was time to go to the Olympic trials. *Coach* was happy that the group had all progressed well over the time they had all been together. He found it amazing that he could not pick between their individual chances of success. It all came down to how they would apply themselves; it was nearly time.

A few weeks before the trials, *Should've* turned up at training not looking his usual fit and healthy self.

"How are you?" a concerned *Coach* asked.

"Not good, *Coach*. I feel tired."

Coach could tell something wasn't quite right and

adjusted the session to accommodate *Should've*'s lack of energy. It wasn't long before *Should've* really began to struggle. It was clear that he was ill.

This was terrible timing, as one of the major steppingstones was to get through the Olympic trials effectively in order to qualify. *Should've* felt really depressed; he thought that his dream was all but over. He knew he needed to be at his best to get through to the finals and into the Olympic team.

Should've had to step back from training for the rest of the week while the others prepared for one of their most important races. This wasn't just another race, they would be running directly towards their future.

This presented both a physical and psychological challenge to *Should've*. This was not how he had chosen to prepare and his inherent inability to change was going to be tested to the limit, now he would not only have to change and adapt to the current situation, but would have to continue to believe in himself as if he'd done things as perfectly as he wanted.

At the trials, *Could've* and *Did* excelled, coming first and second respectively. This was huge, but *Coach* took great pride in all of his athletes and was concerned for the well–being of *Would've* and *Should've*.

Would've had done well, he came fourth but acted like he had won, which worried *Coach* as it was as if he had already reached his dream. This was frustrating, *Would've* seemingly lacked the desire and passion to get himself to the next level.

Coach took the opportunity to talk to *Would've* later that same day, "Have you ever heard of the acronym PMA?"

"Say again, *Coach*?"

"Positive Mental Attitude. Many use it to reference the art of increasing achievement through optimistic thought processes. Well, I'm not mad on the phrase, but we all know what it means. My point is that it is not enough. Hasn't anyone ever told you that in order to get results you need to take *action*?" explained *Coach*.

"Yes, *Coach* ... you! I'm doing the best I can, *Coach*," said a defensive *Would've*.

Coach wanted to steer *Would've* away from confrontation: "Alright, I suppose I walked straight into that one. Look, you know what it takes to be the best you can be. I don't need to tell you that. But – and there is always a *but* – you need to make the best of what you've got. You need to choose your goals and work steadily towards them. But not only that, you need to keep going until you reach them, knowing you'll be a better person for it. And you haven't yet reached your goals, so you need to transform your habits, and adapt your thinking and your behaviour to that of a winning athlete."

Would've said, "So you think I've got more in my tank of reserves?"

Coach replied, "Yes, I do. The vital source of your inner energy is the power of concentration. Staying focused helps to direct your mental power and strength towards the realisation of your dreams. So long as you are focused your tank is full"

"So what about focusing on everything that's going on around me, won't it drain my mind?" asked *Would've*.

"Focus on one goal at a time rather than considering everything at the same time. Like a steam engine, where the pressure builds up through closure of the valves, your focus needs to be concentrated on a single purpose. This single purpose is not here yet, think of that. This way you can focus all of your energy on the objective in front of you. The power of concentration is the driving force that makes some attain success faster than others," answered *Coach*.

"So how much focus do I need to apply to get what I want, *Coach*?" *Would've* asked.

"If you are able to focus unswervingly on your goals, then all that you desire will become yours. The level of your concentration decides the extent of the realisation of your dreams. By focusing all of your energy towards a single goal, you will successfully achieve that goal," said *Coach*.

"I think I'm getting it now," *Would've* muttered.

Coach thought for just a fraction longer than he usually did and said, "All those who have found success in this sport have attained it because of their powerful concentration."

Coach turned his attention to *Should've*; he felt sorry for him, as he had started to change and was beginning to show signs of being a potential champion, adapting and changing his normal routines and executing them effectively. Maybe the trials just came a little too early for him after the recent illness?

Should've, for the first time, thought about the idea of just giving up. He'd tried everything (in his own mind) and it seemed that this was too big a hurdle to conquer. *Should've* remembered back to an earlier training session, the lesson *Coach* had taught them at the time seemed relevant here.

Should've remembered a test which he had dreaded – a fitness test known as the bleep test.

The challenge was to run between two markers, twenty metres apart, at a pace which kept with the timing of a 'bleep', which got quicker and quicker until they either had to stop or couldn't reach the marker before the bleep went off. *Should've* remembered that he perceived the test to be one of physical fitness, but now realised it had a far more important purpose.

Should've recalled, "I remember all four of us starting the test together. *Could've* seemed brave, but had later admitted he was inwardly nervous, which surprised me. *Would've* was reluctant, as it seemed too much like hard work, but he felt some pride in not being exposed as lazy.

"I was apprehensive, purely because I had never seen this test before and I remember your encouragement giving me the courage to explore my boundaries.

"I think *Would've* dropped out first, then *Could've* and I left *Did*, who looked like he was at death's door as he finished. But in a strange way seemed to enjoy it!"

"I remember it well," said *Coach*. "Do you remember *why* you did it, though?"

"Yes, I think so, and it has had a lasting effect on me and my behaviour."

Coach was keen to hear this from *Should've*'s own mouth, discover his interpretation and, hopefully, read in his tone that he'd taken *ownership* of this important trait, so he asked, "What did you learn?"

"Well, *Coach*, throughout your coaching your words have had an enormous impact on me. I have written everything down."

With this, *Should've* pulled a small book from his bag, flicked through the pages and stopped. "Ah, this is it!" *Should've* said proudly.

"May I see?" *Coach* asked.

On a full page, the rule was written out in just the same way *Coach* had seen it in his own mind.

RULE 9
Champions Never Give Up

You must always believe you can succeed. You must go relentlessly in pursuit of this – success, with an unwavering, unfaltering commitment.

Some say it's easy to succeed when everything around you is going well, that may be true. What is certainly true is that it is a lot more difficult to deliver if things are going badly. To retain self–belief and to not give up when all seems to be going wrong is imperative. You have to make things happen and, to do this, you have to carry on believing, and striving, no matter what.

Coach finished with a profound statement. He said...
"Nothing could be any worse than having to turn to your friends, your colleagues and your loved ones and say – 'I gave up too soon'."

Coach noticed that *Should've* had even made further notes.

"What do your notes say?"

"At times, I have caught myself wanting to give in, wanting to revert to perceived comfort in what I think is right but when I feel beaten, I remember this, write it down and it makes me brave. It gives me the confidence to keep searching and to never, ever stop trying. You have taught me this but I feel I have let you down."

"All I ask is that you have given your absolute all; you are not accountable to me," *Coach* said firmly.

Should've suddenly felt vulnerable, as he had begun to depend upon *Coach*.

"You are only accountable to one person and that is the person who looks back at you every time you look in the mirror." *Coach* put his hand on *Should've*'s shoulder. *Should've* sensed that *Coach* was feeling his pain. His dream seemed like it was over, and four years was maybe too long for him to wait for the next Olympic Games.

Coach handed a handwritten '*Coach* Quote' to *Should've* and said, "Keep this with you at all times. When you feel like this again, read it."

COACH QUOTE

Success is simply never giving in to failure – either in mind or body.

Rule 10

Champions have a Calm, Comprehending Nature

'Acting' like a Champion

The results of the Olympic trials...

> *Could've* – 1st
> *Did* – 2nd
> *Would've* – 4th
> *Should've* – Didn't make the final

Could've

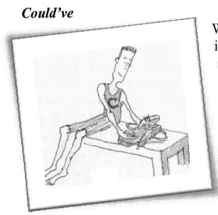

Was feeling particularly inspired; he now wanted success more than ever and was beginning to really believe in himself.

Would've

His passion for success had grown, and he was thankful to *Coach* for helping him see this by helping him understand what was important and to focus on it. This improved clarity was beginning to give *Would've* the purpose and therefore the passion that had been missing

Did

Realised that *Coach* was there to help him, but that, ultimately, it was up to him to take ownership of all the principles that *Coach* had taught him.

Should've

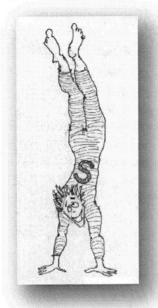

Was left wondering what he 'should' do and would probably admit that he had gone through the motions over the last few days.

The only reprieve would come the following weekend: the closing date for qualifying for the Olympic Games through running inside the qualifying time.

Should've shook off his disappointment and realised that he had one last chance, if he could really pull everything together.

The final preparation session began at the track. *Coach* introduced the evening's work as the athletes arrived, "Okay, guys, I want you to call your own training session tonight. Remember, there are no medals given out in training and I would like something short and sharp, but it is up to you. What would you like to do?"

The group chose their work and *Coach* said, "If you walk into that stadium and act like you are a champion, you will become one and will walk out as a champion."

They had executed their training effectively and *Coach* was pleased with their progress. After the training that evening, while they sat and stretched, he gave them something to think about: "Do you know your body doesn't know the difference between reality and fiction, if you simply pretend and become the character you desire, your body will find a way to make it all happen for you? At first you may need to be like an actor getting into character, but soon it will become part of you and you will not be able to tell the difference."

"What do you mean?" *Would've* asked.

"I'm saying that you go through life playing different characters. When you are at work you are different to when you are at home or when you are out with your friends. You have learned what the appropriate persona is to deal with each situation and show decorum accordingly.

"Your challenge as an athlete is to explore the most appropriate character for you to take on and then to access this state at will. In different states, you will have different abilities and will surprise yourself with the amount of variation.

"What I am saying is simple, get into character, just like an actor would. *Act like a champion, and then become one.*"

"So if I walk around tall, proud as if I have already won – it will make me win?"

"Well, sort of, it will make it as likely as possible," *Coach* replied whilst nodding slowly.

The final Olympic selection meeting of the season was the last chance for *Would've* and *Should've* to make the team.

Could've and *Did* had already qualified but they decided not to just rest on their laurels, although they gave the meet a miss they still put in a few extra training sessions. Even so, they still managed to squeeze in the time to watch the big race.

Race day came, the athletes went through the preparation for the crucial run. Finally, the moment came.

Bang on time, *Would've* and *Should've* settled to their starting blocks at the end of the straight of the track. *Coach* sat with *Did*, and *Could've* muttered under his breath, "Focus, breathe, channel your energy."

"On your marks," the starter announced. "Set …."

Two loud bangs signified a false start and a flag was raised at the athlete in the lane between *Should've* and *Would've*, who exploded with anger – he was out.

"Stay focused, don't let it get to you," *Coach* whispered to himself. Stay calm!"

But *Would've* had very obviously lost his focus. His attention was being directed first at the starter, then another official. *Coach* was pleased he was displaying passion but it was misguided. This, *Coach* knew, was counter–productive.

The commotion caused by *Would've* continued for some time before the remaining athletes once again settled in their starting blocks.

Would've looked twitchy in his blocks and was clearly distracted by the disruption.

"SET …." the starter had them primed and ready to go.

There was tension in the air and no one seemed to be settled.

The athletes again broke before the gun!

Would've had twitched and then drove out of his blocks early. He was out.

"NO!" *Coach* heard *Would've* shout from the other end of the track.

Coach's heart sank; *Would've* had blown it.

He hadn't committed to what *Coach* had said about staying focused, as he didn't really trust it.

Fortunately *Should've* did trust himself. He stood tall, relaxed his neck and shoulders and let a feeling of calm wash over him.

The race started cleanly on the second request, *Should've* took control and ran the race of his life. He was living the experience. He had been given every reason to doubt through his disjointed final preparation but had chosen to carry on believing. He had chosen to behave – like a champion. And he had won the race.

Coach and the others were left to contemplate a bittersweet day – a day that had exposed two very different mindsets.

Coach turned to the two athletes sitting with him, and said, "It's what's behind the eyes."

"What is?" *Could've* asked.

"You can always tell with a true champion, it's in the eyes. The eyes have it. When you look someone in the eye, especially when they are under pressure, you can see deep into their soul. This transparency shows you what is deep inside, the naked truth. Focus, energy, bliss, adaptivity, connection and insight. That's what you have access to when you remember who you are."

In a way, *Coach* was talking to himself, trying to weigh up the mixed emotions he felt for the two athletes who had gone down two very different paths today.

"Battles are won and lost in people's heads," *Coach* muttered. *Did* and *Could've* nodded in agreement; they understood exactly where he was coming from.

"It is the ability to stay calm, to relax and to appear self–assured; does this make sense to you?"

They nodded as *Coach* turned his head and, with a steely gaze, looked them both in the eye and said something pertinent to them both.

"Champions have time, time to think, time to take their preferred action. You must stay centred – focused, in control, balanced and grounded, relaxed but with inner strength; do this by concentrating on breathing."

Although it was a bit of an isolated thing to say, both *Did* and *Could've* got the message.

"In order to become successful, most people work very

hard and take lots of action, yet never attract the success they deserve. Trying to want it more is not enough on its own. Thinking positive thoughts is not enough on its own. Setting goal, after goal, after goal is not enough on its own. Assuming that one massive action will solve everything is not enough. Working harder, though ... that choice is yours.

"The sprint is like life ... blink and you miss it. The habit–breaking process, though, is like running a marathon. Every step you take towards your goal gets you closer to the finish line."

Did and *Could've* went to talk to the other two, to congratulate and console them. They were a team.

The final Olympic selection meeting of the season was now over. It was now up to the selectors to fill both the individual and relay places.

*****

Coach pulled *Did* to one side. "I want you to lead the relay at the Olympics. You and *Could've* are likely to be the key runners in this team and you have it within you to take the lead in this role. I want you to do it. Are you comfortable with this?"

At first, *Did* felt very uncomfortable. He didn't even know who the team would be and therefore what the implications were. He began making excuses so as not to take this on. He smiled to himself, as this reminded him of *Should've*.

The chances were that *Could've* would be one of the athletes on his team and later that day, when *Could've* and *Did* were alone, they discussed the prospect of competing together on the relay team.

"What do you make of this relay? *Coach* wants me to lead it. What do you think?" *Did* asked him.

163

"People trust you. You always know what to do," replied *Could've*.

Did felt proud and didn't know what to say. Although he was a bit of a loner to start with, it had been turned around and now he enjoyed watching others succeed alongside him, something he would once never have imagined, and now visualised the feeling of being responsible for the success of others. He liked the idea of being on a team in this way and that *Could've*, who used to be so destructive, now believed in him.

His focus had been the individual race, but this was a great opportunity and decided to discuss it further with *Coach*.

"I'm not sure about leading this relay, *Coach*. Do you think it will get in the way of my own individual performance?" *Did* asked.

"I think that, when it's all over, you will look back and see it as one of the most important decisions you ever made – to lead the team successfully.

"If you are unsure about the role then simply 'act with conviction' and people will trust you. You must always stay calm and appear self–assured." *Coach* added, "You are the one they look up to!

"The more you think about it, the more chance there is you'll talk yourself out of doing it. It's an endless cycle of procrastination.

"Your conscious mind and your subconscious mind will put up some resistance, will argue with you and try to get you to give up. Don't listen. Forge ahead. Think of how accomplishing what you want will help you improve your life, as you aren't going to be an athlete forever.

"When you shift your focus and when you send your subconscious mind a new set of instructions you begin to attract the people, situations and opportunities to help you achieve your goal.

"The key to successfully overcoming any procrastination lies in the ability to focus. I suggest you formulate a plan for your success and follow that plan.

"Motivation is a dual carriageway, you can choose to be motivated *towards* your goals or *away* from what you don't want. Both options may be considered two sides of the same coin, with both directions being good.

"Why do we regret? It's quite simple really: we don't know where we are going! This happens because we have not identified our core values in life. How can we go where we are supposed to go when we have no clue where we are going or how we will get there? When you have a sense of purpose you will automatically spend more time achieving the goals that will bring you success, prosperity, better health and more."

During the final training sessions of their preparation for the Games, the dynamic began to change - *Coach* was beginning to take even more of a backseat role.

"*Could've*, you looked good today," *Did* remarked while getting changed.

Did was beginning to sound like *Coach* and it wasn't the first time he had noticed this.

Did was really beginning to understand and realise his destiny.

The athletes were nearly ready for their ultimate test and, as *Coach* talked them through their session for the evening workout, he realised that they had, without being prompted, learned a great lesson. *Coach* was delighted to be able to share the tenth rule with them after training:

RULE 10
Champions have a Calm, Comprehending Nature

"You have all begun to behave like champions. You are (mostly) calm and act with conviction.

"You have learned to retain a clear head and an honest perspective. You will, if you choose, be calm even under extreme pressure and as a result, other people will trust you and your opinion. This rule will not only make you great athletes under pressure but will make you incredible role models and, as you grow, it will also make you great leaders."

During the warm–down after the session the following day, the group dialogue, for some unknown reason, turned to Swift. As they drew closer to the Games, it seemed Swift's name was mentioned more and more, and *Coach* saw this as a great motivator into getting them mentally prepared, as Swift was the man to beat. Unwittingly, Swift had become a motivational force amongst the four athletes.

"He seemed really confident to me," said *Could've* about Swift.

"Yeah, self–assured, with vast and varied experience. He's clearly done lots of different things in the past to build a wealth of experience," *Should've* said. "It seems he has also embraced change throughout his career."

"He seemed very passionate, too," *Would've* noted.

Did had noticed how Swift had a calmness in his eyes, a type of silent confidence, without being arrogant. He was self–assured, and was charismatic with this charm and confidence.

All four had seen the same thing but had read it in different ways.

Coach knew that the athletes would be inclined to judge Swift on the same basis on which they judged themselves. *Coach* saw this as a good sign: it meant they had grown in awareness. It became apparent to *Coach* and each of the four athletes that Swift possessed the weakness each of the four athletes have worked hard to overcome and strengthen.

This was close to the end for *Coach,* as the last step would be for them to build this calmness and confidence into their own lives.

He handed each of them another '*Coach* Quote'.

COACH QUOTE

*The only test is what you see
when you look in a mirror.*

RULE 11

Champions Live in the Present

The power of now

Could've and *Did* were really excelling in this, the most important year. *Coach* had received news from the governing body that they had both made the Olympic team to compete as individuals in the 100m. *Coach* also received some news that he could barely believe – due to injuries in one of the other key athletes, all four had qualified for the relay squad. This was a huge success not only for the athletes but for *Coach* too.

He had prepared them well, but the real test was soon to come, namely how they would all cope in the most intense sporting arena of all.

Coach knew that *Could've* would respond well once he'd taken responsibility for his own self–belief, and so he began to challenge him more, almost to test his new resolve and used phrases like: "*Did* really wants to beat you this weekend, you know?"

Could've also began to talk to himself in exactly the same way as *Coach* had taught him. He started to ask himself things like, "Why do I feel so good today?", even if he didn't.

Could've realised that it wasn't a case of coming up with the right answers, it was more a case of coming up with the right questions and trusting himself to solve them. The more he did this, the more his confidence grew.

Could've started sensing the positive results of his efforts when his confidence grew, he was becoming more courageous, stronger. The pessimistic thoughts he once had – that good things only happened to the people around him – had vanished. He was starting to claim ownership of every action, stamping his authority on what he was doing in a slow, natural and deliberate way.

Whilst they were not going to be part of the individual race, *Coach* knew the importance of *Should've* and *Would've* contributing effectively to the squad in order to maintain the momentum for everyone.

Slowly, but surely, *Should've*'s understanding of variety changed. *Coach* had faith in the methods he was using; some just took a little longer to work than others – this was how Coach rationalised Would've's and Should've's positions. They could still be champions by his criteria but needed more time to develop themselves.

Coach was generally delighted that the group had otherwise sharpened their focus on their specific needs and that this had allowed them to develop.

Specifically, *Coach* was pleased that *Should've* had begun to take responsibility for initiating change. *Coach* continued to withdraw his input, his work wasn't quite done, but he realised the importance of stepping away in order to allow the final stage to take place. That final stage was complete ownership of their lives by each of the athletes.

While *Did*'s primary focus was as an individual, there was no greater series of lessons for *Did* than the relay could offer. *Coach* realised that, in order to achieve greatness, there was value in *Did* learning that working together with others could give him the impetus to raise his game.

He'd set *Did* hard sessions on days that he would train alone, and then would repeat the same session as a group. *Did* hated to admit it, but he performed better when he worked with the others and this increased awareness was exactly what *Coach* had wanted. *Coach* hoped that *Did* realised the consequence of not taking ownership of this type of behaviour.

Coach's work was now very nearly completely done. He had taught the athletes a lot, but soon his ability to effect change would be over and it would all be up to them.

"The trust that resides within the team," *Coach* thought to himself, "will be their driving force. To achieve success in life you have to believe in the method and also, essentially, in yourself!"

The team travelled to the Olympic village to do some final preparation.

This was it, the BIG day had finally come.

The day of the individual final was clear and fine, cool at first but the temperature increased as *Coach* walked through the athletes' village to take them for a light breakfast.

Coach had prepared a lengthy speech about how all achievers and extraordinary persons have overcome endless and seemingly impossible hurdles to be where they are now, and how, if you hear each of their stories, the truth of this will be apparent. The obstacles and the lacking they experienced in life did not deter them from reaching their dreams. This is the way one should live: without limitations.

But, instead, he found himself saying, "In reality, there are no limitations. Limitations are changeable into whatever form you want them to take to realise your goals. What you perceive becomes your reality, and when you picture something in your mind, then that is what you create."

Because his athletes *Did* and *Could've* were focusing on the biggest race of their lives, they got only the essence of this important message. This was enough for *Coach*. He appreciated and respected their concentration and left them to apply themselves in a way that felt right for them.

Because of the way *Coach* had learned to understand

each of his athletes, he knew the importance of 'being there' for them when needed but not being too prescriptive, to add too much at inappropriate times, or to distract them with anything that wasn't going to affect their performance positively. This, *Coach* knew at this stage, meant 'less is more' and anything added was only extremely positive in nature. If *Coach* was going to say anything to them, it should be early in this final preparation and then let the two absorb his comments, get into character and focus.

*****

Finally it was nearly time for *Did* and *Could've* to do battle in the individual event.

The pair went to the warm-up track some four hours before the big race.

Soon, it would be time to get ready, to get into character and run through everything they had learned.

Coach came with them, and they could sense that he had something important to say. This was *Coach*'s last chance for any input, before stepping back and allowing them to concentrate fully.

"Let me dispel some often misguided assumptions about delivering under pressure. It is better to be nervous than too calm. It is also better to be scared than over confident, better underprepared than over trained, better fresh than tired, better to be yourself than the person you are expected to be and most of all, better to compete with your heart rather than your head."

A few moments of silence followed to allow the two to absorb what *Coach* had said....

"This is it, guys. You have come a long way, you have prepared well and you have learned many valuable lessons that I hope will stay with you for many years."

Coach paused, but both knew there was more to come and they were keen to hear it: "Everything I have taught you refers to a conscious state of mind that will assist you in building a greater self, a person that is in control of their destiny, in any sphere.

"When it comes to performing in the big arena later today, I want you to forget everything I have told you."

"What?" *Could've* was confused, but thankfully *Coach* continued and made perfect sense: "I want you to trust in yourselves. When you express yourself at the very highest level in sport, it is about letting go of any analytical thinking. It is about trusting yourself and your own ability to perform, you must get out of your own way.

"From now on I want you to have no conscious thought. I want you to clear your minds and live in the moment. Get into and stay in the present."

Coach thought to himself .... "Too often, people get stuck in a state of over–thinking, the result is that they never reach a decision."

Coach then continued, "Well, the first step is the most important. It is the most crucial and the most effective as it will initiate the direction you have chosen. Once you have your plan, run through taking an early and deliberate first step. Just identify the very first physical action you need to take, and do it.

"You don't need to think about it or ponder the consequences. Just do it immediately."

Coach let the two absorb this and continued because he realised they wanted more... "One of the secrets to success is recognising that motivation follows action. The thrust of continuous action is the firewood which fuels motivation. So go out there and act boldly, as if the only thing you can do is win. If you keep adding fuel to your desire, you will reach the point of knowing that you'll achieve ultimate success.

"The first thing to do is to form a candid picture of success in your mind. Visualise your goal and harness a passionate approach.

"As we have rehearsed many times, I want you to get into your most effective performance state, switch it on now. Have you noticed how time can pass quickly sometimes? Maybe at a party, time seems to race on by and you can't keep up? At other times, maybe, when you are on a long journey, time seems to slow down.

"Every great performer I have ever met has the ability to slow things down and to take control of their perceptions.

"True champions are able to retain this clarity while others around them are losing their heads. You might call this being in the *zone*, or in the *flow*.

"You can do this now and it will feel great ….

"Does this all make sense to you right now?"

Did nodded confidently and clearly wanted to talk, so *Coach* stopped. "I believe I can access this state if I really want to."

Could've rolled his eyes.

Did continued, "To me it feels like I have handed over control of my actions to a trusted inner self. I feel completely in control, have total belief, total trust in myself and things seem to fall into place like I am watching myself in a mind movie. I feel invincible."

"I've seen that movie … *Ghostbusters*!" *Could've* quipped.

They all laughed, but they knew that *Did* had something special. He had another gear, another dimension which allowed him to step it up when it mattered. In *Coach*'s mind, this made *Did* a champion already. He hadn't used that word in this context before. But *Did* was special, and even in these final stages was still growing and improving.

The final couple of hours before the race, *Coach* stayed

quiet. He knew they were both ready. The only input he had was an occasional nod of his head, a smile and to stand with the general body language which demonstrated confidence and enthusiasm towards his young prodigies.

Both athletes went smoothly through the qualifying round; *Coach* was delighted.

It was nearly time for the final of the Olympics and *Coach* noticed *Could've* starting to become distracted. There was a jumpiness about him. He seemed edgy and nerves were clearly getting to him.

"Stay focused" *Coach* shouted to *Could've* as he ran past during the warm–up.

He had one last chance to have an input and pulled *Could've* and *Did* to one side at the edge of the warm–up track and explained:

RULE 11
Champions Live in the Present

"You have both learned well and now operate in the here and now when you are in a race. You understand the power of timing and the power of patience. I have noticed that neither of you seem rushed. You know that 'now' is the time that you can control most effectively. When you enter the Olympic stadium, you will feel you have all the time you need, others won't.

"If not you, who? If not now, when?"

Could've and *Did* knew exactly what this meant and the power it would bring.

They also had painful memories of being caught

daydreaming and missing the moment.

Coach said, "When the time comes, it will be like a window of opportunity will open in front of you. Your focus will be on grasping that moment. When it happens, act, be brave and do what you know you can do."

After a few seconds of silence that seemed to last a lot longer, *Coach* continued, "Remember, when you are under pressure, your body and mind may play tricks on you. Your job is to retain your perspective and stay in the here and now, as that is where you can be most effective."

This made sense to the group and they all had to fix this trait securely into their instilled behaviour.

Coach gave them all another '*Coach* Quote'.

COACH QUOTE

Compete like you cannot fail.

Rule 12

Champions Expect More

New mountains to climb

Coach went back to the village once the athletes had entered the call room. This was their time. They were ready and they now had to have the freedom to take control, to take responsibility.

He knew that he could not affect what happened from here on. It was not down to good luck, it was down to all the work they had done and the lessons learned. It was up to his pupils, who had all, in their own way, become champions. Their journeys were nearly complete. They were about to realise their destiny.

Coach never used the words 'good luck': he felt that luck is a force that provides you with prosperity or lets you suffer in poverty. He recalled, with fondness in his heart, the first meeting he'd ever had with the four athletes and how he told them about how they could create their own good luck. Yes, they had come a long way since then!

The luck *Coach* had in mind was the luck that was possessed by an energy. An energy within the person, which could be changed at will by influencing it with positive thought and application.

Putting all thoughts of four–leaf clovers to one side, *Coach* understood that our control over luck is not the only thing that affects it, firstly we have to have belief in ourselves.

Coach joined the other two athletes, *Should've* and

Would've, to watch the race on the large screen. The tension could be felt even miles away, back at the Olympic village.

"They can cope if they can just stay focused, stay in the present and trust themselves," thought *Should've*.

This was the ultimate test for his two finest athletes and *Coach* smiled when he thought about *Could've*'s journey, especially when he remembered the *Could've* he first met: a brash, naive young man, who challenged others in order to cover up his own self–doubt, yet who had transformed himself into someone who was aware and in control. Just as *Coach* had intended, *Could've* had moved from doubting his abilities to standing tall as he faced the ultimate test.

This transformation was as important to *Coach* as to what might happen over the coming moments

Coach recalled one of the first in–depth conversations he'd had with *Could've*: "Always be prepared for sudden changes in your life. The change may occur rapidly, or more slowly. However it may occur, always have your mind open to the happenings in your life."

Should've and *Would've* sat with *Coach*.

"This is painful watching, like we are being punished for not achieving" *Should've* whispered.

"Failure can be the steppingstone to success, and losses can be called 'strengtheners', as they make you more determined to reach your goal.

"You have to create your self–belief by going to your core to find the probable reasons for the negativity in you, and then demolish them.

"Like everything in life, it is not what happens to you but how you respond to it that counts. I suggest you watch the race closely, learn from it and come back a stronger person as a result of what you learn, not only today but along the way," said Coach.

*****

"Look at *Could've*, he looks so proud and focused. He even looks relaxed. Like he's having fun!" *Should've* spilled with excitement.

"I think he is doing as you asked him to, *Coach*. He's breathing from deep within – slowly, shoulders down and back. We know him and what he'll really be feeling, but no one else would know that inside he's a bag of nerves!" *Would've* added.

Coach could take little credit for *Did's* success in making the final, as he had displayed all the basic characteristics he'd wished for since day one. *Coach* merely rounded the hard edges off and put a shine on to *Did's* ability to perform. Nonetheless, *Coach* had worked *Did* very hard and it was a pleasure to see him fit, healthy and looking so ready.

Coach, *Should've* and *Would've* watched on the screen as the finalists stood behind their starting blocks. Both *Could've* and *Did* stood tall and looked like they really meant business.

Coach recalled a conversation he'd had just after meeting *Did*: "If you remain static and wait for success to come to you it will certainly not happen. You have to be aggressive and active, if you want it badly enough. The possibilities open to you will be attainable only through the willpower you have. The action you take decides how quickly your desires will be realised."

It was now all in the execution. They were asked to take their marks at the starting blocks.

"This is it," said *Would've*.

"Set …."

The race began on the first request and was over in a flash; it took photo finishes to work out the positions. At first glance, all *Coach* could tell was that his athletes had coped well and delivered. They were in the mix and had probably run the fastest races of their lives, given the winning time. *Did* was certainly in the mix, just ahead of *Could've*.

The official results appeared on the screen. There was no surprise when the winner was revealed – the ever–fast Swift. Both *Could've* and *Did* had run lifetime bests. One had overcome doubt and eliminated fear to access this level of performance and the other was living proof to *Coach* that his Rules for Success could be learned, taking an athlete to a greater level of performance. *Coach* felt great pride when he saw their finishing positions.

Did took third, *Could've* came fourth: this was a huge success.

The scenes afterwards were mesmerising for *Should've* and *Would've*, and for the first time *Would've* felt a great passion to be there next time, maybe. Seeing his two training partners delivering this level of performance under extreme pressure made *Would've* feel proud, proud for his colleagues but also in himself. It was like the penny had dropped in terms of him understanding his destiny.

Would've turned to congratulate *Coach*, but *Coach* had gone. He had said nothing, but had just left in the commotion at the end of the race.

"Where is he?" *Would've* asked, even though he knew *Should've* didn't know either by the look on his face.

"Maybe he's gone. It kind of feels like the end, eh?"

"I feel like it's just the beginning," *Would've* replied.

Later that evening, *Did* and *Could've* arrived back at the athletes' village. There was no time to celebrate, the relay was tomorrow, so they were keen to discuss tactics with *Coach*.

They were greeted by *Would've*: "*Coach* has gone, he just upped and left. We thought he might come back, but then we found this note and a '*Coach* Quote' on each of our beds."

I am proud of all of you, you have all strived and given 100%; for this, I am grateful. My work is done now. Thank you for allowing me to work with you all. I leave you with one final rule:

RULE 12
Champions Expect More

Champions strive to deliver their maximum and take responsibility in raising the bar to the next level. You are all now champions in my mind, and as a result will constantly look to develop all aspects of your performance.

It is true to say that the secret of a winning formula is the ability to accept that there is a vast area of unexploited potential beyond what you currently perceive to be your maximum.

You must expect more of yourself and of those around you. You will actively encourage others to explore beyond perceived boundaries, to push hard and reach for new levels. When this is done in a positive and honest way, growth and development happens every day.

Remember the magic of alignment and compete like you cannot fail.

6All felt a greater responsibility to deliver in the relay, they owed this to *Coach*.

They were surprised that he was gone and were not even sure if they would see him again. Even before the race, it had felt like they had reached their destiny. They were all eternally grateful to *Coach* and knew that they owed him the greatest service of all – to work as a team.

It almost seemed like the 'extra' bit that came as a result of them working together was *Coach*'s spirit. This is the bit that he had left them with, and they were determined to capitalise on this.

The final '*Coach* Quote' was fitting and drew some emotion from the four.

COACH QUOTE

If you want to continue to be the best in the world, then you have to train and compete like you are second best in the world.

Did recalled how *Coach* had asked each one of them to write about their experiences, one of the many writing exercises he had given them when they first joined the group. He said, "I think now is the time for reflection."

Could've

When I joined the group, I now realise, I was lacking belief; I had no self–confidence. I became aware of this and started to work on it. It developed.

Should've

When I first joined, I really didn't like new ideas. I was unaware that the routines I lived under were holding me back. I thought that they made me disciplined. I then became aware and began to explore and adapt to change.

Would've

When I joined, I lacked passion and I had no motivation for getting stuck in — to be focused. I learned that this can be tackled through clarity and understanding personal values.

Did

When I joined the group, I didn't realise I'd get more from a group environment. My destiny was in helping others through using the magic of alignment, I realise this is now my chosen responsibility.

The four met up that evening to discuss how they could raise their bar to the highest possible level, act as a true team and apply *Coach*'s 'Magic of Alignment'. They went through everything they had learned from *Coach*.

Should've created a positive thought when he said to himself, "I have the instinctive feeling that remarkable things are going to happen to me. Something really incredible is going to take place today, this day, the day of the relay race at the Olympic Games."

Did interrupted *Should've*'s flow of thought when he said, "I remember when *Coach* first arrived, when he took us to the mountain. Do you remember? We all thought he was a bit mad, but he taught us:

RULE 1
Champions decide to work hard
"We have done this. We have all worked very hard a nd deserve to be here. I am proud to have had the pleasure of working with you all. Especially you, *Could've!*"

RULE 2
Champions have great awareness
"We now all know and accept our strengths and weaknesses. As a group, we look out for each other. We have a greater awareness as individuals too."

RULE 3
Champions give their dream a higher purpose
"This is our dream, we are living it. Many athletes talk of sacrifice, as if they'd rather be doing something else. I must say, there was no sacrifice for me: I have looked forward to every session that we have done in pursuit of where I now am – living my dream."

RULE 4
Champions have PRIDE – Personal Responsibility in Delivering Excellence
"It is up to us now. This is our collective responsibility. Together, we can be far greater than the sum of our parts ... if we trust in the 'Magic of Alignment'."

RULE 5
Champions have clarity of vision and a clear purpose
"We are in lane 5; I want you all now to each see yourself

standing in your lane, ready. I want you all to see it, feel it and trust it. Feel the spikes on your feet, the warm breeze on your face and the noise of the crowd in the stadium. Feel the speed of the movement and be the baton. See the lane ahead of you with a bright light in it: that will give you energy to explode forward. This will allow you to stay focused. We must stay focused."

RULE 6
Champions challenge the process
"We have learned to do things differently and have learned to ask 'why' when appropriate. Now it is time to trust our process, not to challenge it anymore."

It occurred to *Should've* that *Did* was sounding more and more like *Coach*.

RULE 7
Champions take action
"We would normally wait for *Coach*, but now we will have to step up and do it for ourselves; maybe this is what *Coach* wants from us? *Coach* always liked it when we took action without being prompted; well now he's got it."

RULE 8
Champions are always keen to learn, keen to enquire and keen to listen and understand
"We have learned from the best, and this has been of huge benefit to us. The next step is for us to believe and trust that we can actually be better than our competitors. We must take it to the next level."

RULE 9
Champions never give up

"Others have fallen, we will fight on. Run with your heart and your soul; run like you have never run before."

RULE 10
Champions have a calm, comprehending nature
"Many people, having seen us train together as a group, tell us that we have a sense of calmness, that the energy is powerful around us. When we are together, it is inspirational. If we can channel this positive energy, we can beat anyone."

RULE 11
Champions live in the present
"Here and now, over the next day or so, we will decide our future. Some of us have already had a taste of being in the stadium individually. We know what to expect and this time we have each other, in order to be even greater."

RULE 12
Champions expect more
"We can win. If we believe it enough, we can do it. We must be able to see it in our minds, feel it in our bones and trust in those images and feelings."

"Are we all okay and one–hundred per cent aligned? Let's take this to the next level." *Did* stopped, closed his eyes and saw himself in the race, the others followed. They were beginning to position themselves to do something special. They knew that it was now up to them to apply all of these traits simultaneously – to live in the present with the Magic of Alignment.

"I want you all to remember ... a champion team will always beat a team of champions."

It was as if this had come straight from *Coach*'s mouth.

*****

The day of the relay race was here and the guys knew what was needed. They were well–prepared and disciplined.

The lane draw was fortuitous, putting them one lane inside the reigning champions.

The team went together for breakfast and shared some relaxed banter and their personal stories about *Coach*. He had touched them all in some way and they all knew how the others felt about him without saying so.

Did had taken the role of team leader for this relay, and discussed each of the scenarios that could unfold and how they would each react.

What they needed to do was to focus on running their race and staying focused, whatever else was might be going on around them.

They sat together for the short bus ride to the stadium and put their bags in the same part of shade before starting their warm–up routine.

It was obvious to the other teams that they had a real sense of togetherness as they jogged in formation, exchanging the baton back and forth, up and down the line. They were so well–aligned, other coaches even remarked at how 'ready' they seemed.

The teams were called to check in and the four athletes went out into the arena, de–robed, and went into the stadium and to their respective corners of the track. It was as if no one else existed.

*****

The Race

This was the BIG event. They were all keyed-up; this was the culmination of all their previous efforts.

As the more popular athletes were recognised by the crowd, they erupted into screams and cheers.

Coach's four were in lane 5, while Swift's team was running in lane 6.

The race was underway. Swift's team had a slender lead at the first handover, although it was a wobbly change as the baton went to the second runner at the start of the back straight. However, *Should've* had ran a great first leg and the baton change with *Could've* was slick.

Could've knew he had to believe and run with all his heart if he were to keep his team's chances of a podium place alive.

Down the long straight, at the far side of the stadium, Swift's second runner was now losing ground to lane 4's runner. This kept the race even, as *Could've* knew he would stay ahead of lane 4 before the stagger would unwind.

As the third leg runners prepared to take the batons, ready to run the second bend, it was neck and neck between lanes 3 and 4.

Lane 4 fumbled and lost some ground, leaving *Would've* on the third leg with only the two teams from lanes each side of him now just slightly ahead. Between them, *Could've* and *Would've* were focused and trusted one another. The changeover was fluent and gave *Would've* great momentum for running the bend.

Swift's team looked to be going strong, and were just in the lead, although fumbled slightly in the final change. The runner in lane 4 made a bid for the lead, but mistimed the changeover and disaster struck! He ran into the back of his team mate and dropped the baton!

Did was about to be running head to head with Swift on the last leg. For some strange reason, as he waited for the baton, a thought came to him from out of the blue. He recalled something *Coach* had said to him during a training session: "To become a champion is to be a permanent inspiration to others. If obstacles along the way seem large, jump higher. Reach for the stars."

Did started his run, put his hand back and felt the baton in his hand; he was off like a rocket. Perfect!

Did knew that he could settle for second place, or he could really compete. This was when he had to dig deep ... and he chose to compete.

Due to the dropped baton by the pre–race favoured team in lane 4, *Coach*'s team were now promoted into second place.

Swift was running half a stride ahead of *Did*, and thought to himself, "All you have to do is hold him off."

Around the halfway mark of the final leg of the race, *Did* recalled the 'beat me' challenge from Swift: how he would give generously to a charity of his choice if he managed to beat him.

Did recalled one of the very first things *Coach* had said to him: "You need to draw strength from others." The roar of the crowd let Swift know *Did* was coming up gradually....

As *Did* drew level with Swift, he felt the presence of *Coach* and thought to himself, "If not you, who? If not now, when?"

The two were neck and neck as they both lunged for the line, together ... a photo finish.

The athletes slowed gradually, there was great suspense. Swift said to *Did*, "I don't think your charity is in line for a donation ... I've got it in the bag!"

Did was calm on the outside, but inside his heart was pumping hard.

It was a full five minutes before the photo finish decision was made. Tension mounted in the crowd in anticipation of the final result, which was close. After what seemed like an age, the athletes were still unsure who had taken the medals.

Finally, the results flashed up on the giant stadium screens, and simultaneously an announcement came over the PA system: "In first place, and with a new Olympic record ...."

Swift was visibly crestfallen at what he heard.

As it dawned on *Did* that it was his team that had won, he jumped into the air with a scream that could be heard around the whole stadium, and was soon joined by his jubilant team mates.

Swift was sportsman–like in congratulating *Did* and said, "Hey, when you get the cheque, I want a rematch! Well done, Champ!"

The team of four humble guys had achieved what they set out to do. Four ordinary people had done something extraordinary. This was the realisation of a dream and the culmination of many years of hard work and the efficient application of *Coach's twelve rules for success.*

What would go down as possibly the most memorable race ever was not just a two–horse race between Swift and *Did*, however. This was something that had brought five people together in a common bond of shared identity. Indeed, the whole had been greater than the sum of its parts through utilising the Magic of Alignment.

For all their weaknesses and human frailties, each athlete had contributed to making the team a strong, singular unit. As they talked to each other about the win, they were using the pronouns 'us' and 'we'.

As the four stood huddled as one man on the rostrum to

receive their medals, basking in their glory, they all knew that the gold medal really belonged to *Coach*. This was his success. They hoped he was enjoying his moment, wherever he was.

Afterword

What happened next?

To their friends: *Could've* was now known as *Can*, *Should've* as *Shall* and *Would've* as *Will*.

The most important thing was that the four athletes, because of their openness, had laid down in history a blueprint for any aspiring performer to learn from their individual and collective journey.

Did went into coaching, he saw this as a way he could extend the legacy of *Coach* and allow others to learn from that great man.

Coach was now a granddad and had retired from coaching so he could spend time with his new grandson, who had been christened with the first names of ... *Could've Should've Would've Did.*

Swift had enlisted the services of March so that he could up his game and secure a rematch with *Did*, who was now, like Swift, a household name.

What *Coach* had said to *Did*, just before introducing them to Swift all that time ago, was a self–fulfilling prophecy: "Now you have the chance to learn from him ... and become one of them yourself ... a champion."

Other Titles by Mirage Publishing

Paperback Non-fiction Books
A Prescription from The Love Doctor: How to find Love in 7 Easy Steps - Dr Joanne 'The Love Doctor' Coyle
Burnt: One Man's Inspiring Story of Survival - Ian Colquhoun
Cosmic Ordering Guide - Stephen Richards
Cosmic Ordering: Sex Energy - Stephen Richards
Cosmic Ordering: You Can be Successful - Stephen Richards
Hidden Secrets: Attract Everything You Want! – Carl Nagel
Internet Dating King's Diaries: Life, Dating and Love – Clive Worth
Life Without Lottie: How I survived my Daughter's Gap Year - Fiona Fridd
Forgiveness and Love Conquers All: Healing the Emotional Self - Stephen Richards
Rebel Diet: They Don't Want You to Have It! – Emma James
The Real Office: An Uncharacteristic Gesture of Magnanimity by Management Supremo Hilary Wilson-Savage - Hilary Wilson-Savage
The Tumbler: Kassa (Košice) – Auschwitz – Sweden - Israel - Azriel Feuerstein (Holocaust survivor)
Uncle Hitler: A Child's Traumatic Journey through Nazi Hell to the Safety of Britain – Alfred Nestor

Paperback non-fiction books – Mrs Darley Series
Mrs Darley's Moon Mysteries: A Celebration of Moon Lore and Magic – Carole Carlton

Reality- Stephen Richards

Cosmic Ordering: Sex Energy - Stephen Richards

Develop Jedi Self-Confidence: Unleash the Force within You - Stephen Richards

Forgive or Kill - Stephen Richards

Hidden Secrets: Attract Everything You Want! – Carl Nagel

Internet Dating King's Diaries: Life, Dating and Love – Clive Worth

Life Without Lottie: How I survived my Daughter's Gap Year - Fiona Fridd

Love Magic – manifest love in 7 days – **The Love Doctor**

Overcoming Procrastination - Stephen Richards

Overcoming Self-Limiting Beliefs – Stephen Richards

Releasing You from Self-limiting Beliefs - Stephen Richards

Supercharge Your Self-confidence – Stephen Richards

The Real Office: An Uncharacteristic Gesture of Magnanimity by Management Supremo Hilary Wilson-Savage - Hilary Wilson-Savage

Think Your way to Success: Let Your Dreams Run Free – Stephen Richards

Uncle Hitler: A Child's Traumatic Journey through Nazi Hell to the Safety of Britain – Alfred Nestor

See these titles at:
www.miragepublishing.com www.cosmicordering.net